M000158413

KILL, SLEEP, REPEAT

A PSYCHOLOGICAL THRILLER

BRITNEY KING

WWW.BRITNEYKING.COM

ALSO BY BRITNEY KING

Room 553

Room 553 is a standalone psychological thriller. Vivid and sensual, Room 553 weaves a story of cruelty, reckless lust, and blind, bloody justice.

HER

HER is a standalone psychological thriller which covers the dark side of female relationships. But equally—it's about every relationship anyone has ever had they knew was terrible for them. It's for those of us who swam for the deep end anyway, treading water because it seemed like more fun than sitting on the sidelines. It's about the lessons learned along the way. And knowing better the next time. Or not.

The Social Affair | Book One
The Replacement Wife | Book Two
Speak of the Devil | Book Three
The New Hope Series Box Set

The New Hope Series offers gripping, twisted, furiously clever reads that demand your attention, and keep you guessing until the very end. For fans of the anti-heroine and stories told in unorthodox ways, *The New Hope Series* delivers us the perfect dark and provocative villain. The only question—who is it?

Water Under The Bridge | Book One
Dead In The Water | Book Two
Come Hell or High Water | Book Three
The Water Series Box Set

The Water Trilogy follows the shady love story of unconventional married couple—he's an assassin—she kills for fun. It has been compared to a crazier book version of Mr. and Mrs. Smith. Also, Dexter.

Bedrock / Book One

Breaking Bedrock / Book Two

Beyond Bedrock / Book Three

The Bedrock Series Box Set

The Bedrock Series features an unlikely heroine who should have known better. Turns out, she didn't. Thus she finds herself tangled in a messy, dangerous, forbidden love story and face-to-face with a madman hellbent on revenge. The series has been compared to Fatal Attraction, Single White Female, and Basic Instinct.

Around The Bend

Around The Bend, is a heart-pounding standalone which traces the journey of a well-to-do suburban housewife, and her life as it unravels, thanks to the secrets she keeps. If she were the only one with things she wanted to keep hidden, then maybe it wouldn't have turned out so bad. But she wasn't.

Somewhere With You / Book One

Anywhere With You / Book Two

The With You Series Box Set

The With You Series at its core is a deep love story about unlikely friends who travel the world; trying to find themselves, together and apart. Packed with drama and adventure along with a heavy dose of suspense, it has been compared to The Secret Life of Walter Mitty and Love, Rosie.

COPYRIGHT

Hot Banana Press
Cover Design by Britney King LLC
Cover Image by Britney King LLC
Photo by Stasyuk Stanislav
Copy Editing by Librum Artis Editorial Service
Proofread by Proofreading by the Page

First Edition: 2020
ISBN 13: 9781657640597

britneyking.com

For Hannah, who was a better person than I am even though she was a dog

KILL, SLEEP, REPEAT

BRITNEY KING

"Everything that needs to be said has already been said. But, since no one was listening, everything must be said again." - André Gide

PROLOGUE

The first time it happened, I did not think it was funny. It wasn't funny the second time, either. By that point, saving her ass had become a full-time job. With mandatory overtime. By then, I'd realized something profound—what didn't kill me only made me want her more.

Maybe it would have helped if she'd wanted it. Who's to say?

She may not have wanted to be saved, but God did she need it. And anyhow, what was I supposed to do? Once you've committed to a person on that level, how can you not see it through?

You could say that's what I'm doing now. Seeing it through. The worst thing would be if this was all for nothing. And since I have your attention, this is important, so listen up—what you have here is a story about how everything went south. Not literally south, but what you would call the opposite of right. Upside down. Topsy-turvy. You probably catch my drift.

This thing you're listening to, the flight recorder, well, I bet the boys at the NTSB had a blast fishing it out of the frigid depths of the Pacific. The black box, it's called. In reality, it's orange. Probably my first big point: most things aren't what they seem.

Anyway, on the inside of the black box is the record of all that is left. What you've found is just that. A story about how things went from bad to worse.

Except for one—two, if you count me, which most people don't—the passengers are fine. They deplaned in Dallas, on schedule. Then it was just the two of us. Exactly as it should be.

You really have no idea what it takes to get her alone.

The pilots are with her too.

Although, they don't count. They're dead.

So, it's just me up here in the cockpit. Well, me and a dispensary of half-empty pill bottles. Xanax, Valium, codeine, Adderall— pretty much anything you could want— I have it all lined up in a neat little row on top of the instrument panel.

Maybe it's worth mentioning, I'm not usually this laid back. I don't typically fly while under the influence, but this is what you could call a special circumstance.

Up here, where the air is thin, there's just us trying to stay above the weather.

Well, at least one of us is trying.

The other one is all sad-eyed and what you could call emotional. Could be the zip ties. It's not the first time I've been accused of taking things too far.

That and well...she doesn't particularly care for the term "hostage." Obviously, this is more than that—if anyone has been the captive in this whole ordeal, it's me. Could be, too, that she's thinking about her children. They'll be fine. I did my best to reassure her. They're old enough to make their own food, tie their own shoes. They have a spare parent. Not everyone is so lucky, I said. Not everyone gets to have two.

She didn't seem comforted by this, but then, she's always had a bit of a poker face.

I'll do my best not to bore you with the details, but we're on autopilot up here until we eat through the fuel. Flame out being the technical term.

I won't waste your precious time, or mine, for that matter, by giving you a crash course on the fuel consumption specs of two Rolls Royce jet engines, full throttle at forty thousand feet, or how long it takes a sixty thousand pound glider to harpoon the Pacific Ocean.

Thankfully, I can enjoy the ride down hands free. The autopilot will perform its best dead-stick descent.

What a relief. I can't think of anything I'd rather have.

All I've known since she walked into my life has worked out exactly the opposite.

But I'm probably getting ahead of myself.

For now, the sky expands forever out in front of us. I'm on cloud nine. We have never been more together. Together, headed toward the Pacific, headed toward disaster, toward the end of our life stories, hers and mine, and I suppose all roads really do lead west.

For the record, I have never felt more fantastic.

At this speed and altitude, we have two, maybe three hours left. Which means I'll have to make this quick. No one wants to die in the middle of their life story.

Earlier, as I carefully positioned the dead captain and copilot in their final, seated, upright positions, next to her, she demanded to know why I'm doing this. Believe me, I asked myself the same thing. It took a lot of work getting them into those seats.

In the end, it was worth the effort. It seemed like she had a lot to talk about, and I didn't want her to be lonely.

Still, I didn't answer her, at least not right away, because we both know why. When this thing crash-dives into the Pacific and breaks into a bazillion tiny bits of fiery jet, the black box will survive. Sooner or later, people will find it. So eventually I told her the truth: I'm recording this so our story will live on forever.

CHAPTER ONE

Charlotte

Three weeks earlier

The Uber driver drops me three blocks from my destination. Even though it's a balmy twenty-seven degrees Fahrenheit, I'm more than happy to walk the remainder of the way.

My phone chimes as I step off the curb, a reminder I'd better chuck it. Glancing at the screen, I see a notification asking me to leave a rating on my experience with the driver. Considering his incessant attempts at making small talk are half the reason I'm walking several blocks in five-inch heels, against the bitter cold, I have a few things to say.

I power the phone off, watching as it falls to the pavement, where I channel my frustration into smashing it into bits and pieces with my left foot. No point in shitting on a person's livelihood because I've had a bad day.

Once I've buttoned my coat, I shuffle the broken phone toward the gutter with the toe of my black pump. One small kick and it's a goner, and then I'm on my way. My mind is, as usual, already two steps ahead, welcoming the time to regroup. It's imperative I'm in the right headspace for what I'm about to walk into.

There are three rules. More than that, but three main ones: Stay focused. Remain in character. Don't get murdered.

Head down, I walk briskly toward my destination, my hands in my pockets, the rest of me shivering against the icy breeze, trying to keep the cold air at bay. Pushed back from the road, the house is conveniently situated at the end of a long drive, gated and hidden among trees, away from inquisitive eyes.

It's dark now, but I don't need daylight to know the expansive front lawn is well tended, that there are eight steps to the front door, or that the drive has recently been repaved.

Nor am I surprised to see the walk is well-lit or that the smaller yard up close to the house is littered with toys, tricycles, and various sporting equipment. My host has people for this, so my sense is he's trying to send a message. He wants me to feel safe here. But I know better.

I know that would be a mistake.

It could be this—or it could be that he really doesn't care one way or the other.

Maybe it's a little of both.

Maybe it doesn't matter.

With the exception of a small bench, I know that the porch is empty. To the left of the bench are two pairs of gardening clogs— one adult size, one child size—and next to them, a potted rose bush and a bag of fresh soil.

As I pass the first camera, positioned appropriately along the walk, I smile. Watching is a fetish of his. There are others, but voyeurism makes him feel big and powerful. It makes him feel safe and in control. Funny, a security system, no matter how sophisticated, isn't going to save him tonight.

My heels click purposefully against the porch steps as I make my way toward the front door. I see that the curtains have been left open, a flickering bluish glow emanating from the large front window. As I approach the entryway, I hear a pundit's voice coming from the television inside. It's late, but he's expecting me, and I know he'll have waited up.

I raise a gloved hand, take a solid breath, and allow my fist to rap against the door. I knock three times, the sound dampened by thick leather. Eventually, I hear footsteps, and the door opens. He leans out, holding the door half-closed to keep the cold out, and I have to admit he looks exactly as I pictured him. Handsome. Charming, even. Like someone I could fall in love with, if I didn't know so much about him. If I were capable of such things.

He looks at me, partly confused, partly perturbed. The TV is louder now, one of those urgent, the sky is falling news reports playing on a seemingly endless loop. His eyes are tired, but he hasn't changed out of his work attire. His tie is only slightly loosened. Slowly, he relaxes his grip on the door. "I didn't think you were going to show."

We stand there for a second, staring at each other. I'm thinking he's a good lover. His kind usually are. There's a hunger in his expression I recognize, one I know will tighten its grip unless satisfied.

After several beats, he opens the door wider, beckoning me in. I follow him into the foyer, which screams the usual look-at-me, look-how-much-money-I-have rhetoric, only with too much white space. I change my mind. I bet he's selfish in the sack.

When I see that the living room isn't much different, it's practically confirmed. If given the opportunity to look around, I know what I'd find. Nine bedrooms, eleven bathrooms, three stories, with two boat slips down at the dock. Sure as shit, the rich know how to live: jewelry, guns, clothes, pills of all kinds, loads of money, and plenty of food. But that's not what gets me off. It's always their fetishes I find most interesting.

He doesn't ask for my coat or make a move to remove it, so I take it upon myself. As I lay it over the sofa, I am reminded why I am here. I have two main goals. The most important is to walk out the door alive. Which is why when he asks me if I want a drink, I don't answer. My attention is on the couch. It's the ugliest I've ever seen, rich people or no.

He walks over to the bar and fills a glass with whiskey. Once he tops off a second glass, he turns to me and says, "The dress I like. But what's with the gloves?"

"It's cold out."

"This should warm you up." He forces the tumbler in my direction.

When I neither respond nor move to take it from him, he turns toward the TV. I clock him with a left hook. He drops the glass, the caramel colored liquid soaking into the kind of plush white carpet no one with kids should ever own. Blood seeps from his bottom lip as he lunges forward. He swings as hard as he can but I dart aside, coming back with a knee to the chin that has him on the floor before he knows what's happening. He spits blood as he tries to rise, but I can see in his eyes there isn't a lot to give.

In a single beat, I'm on top of him, straddling his chest. As I reach for my knife, the tips of my fingers grazing it, he shifts his weight, which causes me to side-swipe my hip with the blade. Suddenly, his hands are on my thighs. He squeezes hard. Our eyes meet and I see it then. He thinks this is a game. He thinks it's part of the act.

"So you like it rough," he says. It's not a question. Something that is quickly apparent in the way he bucks me off and back-hands me, once he's succeeded.

Using the back of the horrid sofa, he manages to pull himself upright. He lands another blow. This time it's a fist to my head. I'm slumped forward, propped up by my forearms, when his elbow comes down between my shoulder blades, forcing me all the way down. It knocks the wind out of me, but ignites a fire somewhere deep within. "Why is it the best whores," he says smugly, "always put up a little fight?"

I feel him moving behind me and then he's close. His weight presses me into the plush white carpet. "Look what you've done," he says, kissing my ear, his erection pushing against my back. I shift, trying to get the knife in a position that won't be useless. With his weight pinning me, it's impossible. I reach around and jab my finger into his eye.

He rears backward long enough to allow me to turn onto my back. We roll several times as he gets a few hits in. Finally, he pulls me up by my hair, and that's when he learns that even the best of wigs don't stay put under that kind of stress. "Not even a redhead," he says, shaking his head. I take two steps backward, defeat in my eyes.

He tosses the wig aside and then leans forward, resting his hands on his knees. He tries to catch his breath.

Blood drips from my nose, and I stagger a little as I attempt to regain my footing. The heels don't help.

He sighs heavily, surveying the mess. He motions at my injuries. "Is that enough for you—or should I keep going?"

I don't have time to answer. Suddenly, he's standing in front of me. Suddenly, he's forcing me to my knees, my hair twisted around his fist. With his free hand, he unzips his pants.

I'm aware that I'm in a bad position, but my mind is clear and my hands are steady. He removes his shirt, slowly, button by button. Using my mouth, I snake my way up his torso. I pause and take him in. "Where are the girls?"

"The who?"

"The girls."

He takes my head in his hands and tilts it from side to side as he studies my face. He could easily snap my neck at any moment and I think he just might. "How the fuck should I know?"

Shaking my head loose, I lean forward and nuzzle his stomach. "He said I should talk to you. If I was interested."

"Me? No. You'll have to ask Dunsmore."

"Dunsmore," I repeat, cupping his balls. I stroke the length of him, first with my hand, and then with the tip of my tongue. Eventually his head lolls back and his eyes close. He's in the zone now, the place where expectancy and ecstasy meet in the dark, like a swirling tide, leaving him exposed.

His blood splatters beautifully against the white space, the cut to his throat clean and precise. With a confused look in his eye, he staggers forward.

I smile, knowing he'll bleed out in seconds. That the job is done.

The thrumming sound of my pulse beating between my ears picks up pace as I watch him fall to the floor and then take his last breath.

Kneeling down next to him, I lift the knife to his chest, stopping and hovering just above his rib cage. Using the tip, I trace the word *liar* into the tanned, taut skin above his heart. Then I plunge the blade deep into his chest, erasing everything. I stab again and again, until I hit bone, until I feel nothing, until I'm slumped over him, breathless.

A familiar sensation washes over me, and I sigh, once again reminded that this is what it feels like. *Bliss.* Sweet, fleeting bliss.

When my breath steadies, I stand and compose myself, tucking the knife inside my dress. Then I make my way into the kitchen, where I locate the computer monitor that displays the footage from the cameras. I watch for movement. I see nothing. In the living room, the pundit on the TV is still rambling. I follow the sound back to my drink. I'm pleased to see the ice cubes haven't watered it down. I take the glass and make my way over to the horrible couch, where I stand for a second, sipping the whiskey, taking it all in. I wonder what was going through their minds.

Was it a fad purchase? Or a beloved piece carefully selected with this room in mind?

Maybe a little of both.

Maybe it doesn't matter.

I glance over at the lifeless body sprawled out on the floor, his pants pathetically around his ankles, and I smile. Then I make myself comfortable. And I finish off my drink.

CHAPTER TWO

Charlotte

T he clock on his side of the bed reads 5:47 a.m. Predawn
light filters ever so slightly through the tops of the blackout
curtains. He is on top of me, pumping away. Our Wednesday
ritual.

Sex is important in any marriage, so when Michael suggested
putting it on the calendar, I found no reason to object. Between
my flight schedule, his commute, and two children pulling us in
every direction but the same one, Wednesday, predawn, was the
only available calendar slot.

Seven minutes ago, when the alarm sounded, and he rolled
over to my side of the bed, sweeping his hand across my thigh, I
smiled. Michael is nothing if not punctual. Sure, I'd prefer coffee
over rigorous thrusting first thing, but I admit it's not the worst
thing I could be doing.

Feeling him search for my hands in the dark, I offer up a soft
moan. A distraction, so that the slight crook in the pinky finger

on my left hand, and the nasty greenish-blue hue it has taken on, can remain safely tucked under the pillow.

Eventually, he finds it, and as he does, he shifts his weight, which causes my breath to catch. He takes this as a sign to increase speed, and all of a sudden, I hate myself for breathing. "Flip over," he huffs, pulling out. "I want you from the back."

Gritting my teeth, I methodically roll over. Michael has always loved my ass, it's one of the few things time, gravity, and child-bearing haven't touched. The dim light doesn't hurt.

He sees only what he wants to see.

White-hot heat sears down my lower back when he grabs my left hip, flirting with the bruises that have bloomed across my thighs overnight, anchoring me into position. He sighs, his breath heavy and hot against my ear. "God, you feel good."

He doesn't mean to hurt me. In the dark, it's impossible to make out the telltale signs that adorn my body. In the dark, like other aspects of my life, this, too stays hidden.

Liar. My mind flashes back to letters etched into a tan, hair-less chest, spelling out a word I know well. Gripping Michael's forearm, I dig my nails in. Suddenly, he is not my husband. Suddenly, he is every man who has ever hurt me. Pain is equally intoxicating and suffocating in that way. The body doesn't easily forget.

"Jesus, Charlotte." He slows and runs his fingers up my side, stopping at my face, where he uses them to pry my hand away. "That's going to leave a mark."

His voice brings me back to the present. "Sorry."

"Are you okay? It seems—"

"I'm fine."

I'm not fine. Overnight the bruising that spans my torso has spread upward, snaking itself around my rib cage like vines climbing a trellis. Every breath is a reminder.

"Maybe you'd feel better if you let me take this off," he says, fisting the old T-shirt of his I've refused to remove.

"It's cold." *It's the only thing keeping the laceration on my hip covered.*

His eyes dart toward the clock. "I'll warm you up," he says. And he does. The pain comes cyclically, in waves with each thrust. It radiates angrily, building and subsiding, starting at the base of my forehead, traveling to the tips of my toes, and back again. My body, when pressed into the mattress, aches to let go, to give up, to give in to the pain, or the pleasure, or both. My mind, on the other hand, begs to tell him to slow down. So as not to prolong the session, I bite my tongue. The sweet-metallic taste of blood fills my mouth, keeping me in the here and now.

As he picks up pace, it helps to imagine the faces of men long dead. Slack jaws, lifeless eyes, ridged extremities. It's meant to serve as a distraction, and for a moment, I feel a familiar heat building within me. I think I might actually come.

Unfortunately, the feeling dies just as quickly as it builds. Last night is still too fresh in my mind and clearly also in my body. I can't get there. Wherever *there* is, it remains elusive, a place I know well but remains just out of reach. I can't quite bring it into focus.

Unable to remain in this position without suffocating or crying out, I shimmy back onto my side.

"On your stomach," he says. "Turn over. All the way." It's a half-hearted request, and thankfully, he does not stop to give me the chance to oblige. His hand pushes my hip into the mattress. "Char—"

Instinctively, I sink my teeth into his hand, an act of aggression that is met by one of his own. He twists my hair around his fist and pulls. It makes me smile. He wants to play. That side of him doesn't usually come out this early. "I said turn over."

"No."

He tries to force me, which nicks an edge somewhere deep inside. The impulse to fight is there—the urge to reach for the knife, or the gun under the mattress, to make it stop. But then he slips his hands between my legs, where his fingers begin a delicate dance, and logic prevails. "That feels good..." My fingers grip the sheets. "I'm almost there."

My lie has the intended effect. He speeds up.

"*Oh God.*" He pushes my face into the pillow. "*Oh fuck. Yes. Please. Just—*"

"I'm going to come," he grunts. "I'm—"

In waves at first, and then all at once, his body is rigid, and then it goes slack. After several long seconds, he collapses onto me. "Did you get there?"

"Of course," I say. "Wasn't it obvious?"

"Just wanted to make sure."

There is pleasant relief when he lifts up and climbs off me, and I allow my eyes to close, just for a moment.

I hear him towel off and then the room floods with purple light as he flings the curtain open. He walks back over to the bed and stands there for a second. When I open my eyes, his brows are knitted. After a second or two, he leans down and pats my ass. "What a way to start the day."

As he makes his way across the bedroom and into the bath, I admire all the ways in which middle age has left him relatively unscathed. He's still long and lean and fit, and aside from a few laugh lines and a smattering of crows' feet, not much has changed since the day we met. "You got back late," he says, glancing over his shoulder. "It's no wonder you're tired."

I'm not sure if it's meant to be a dig about my performance or merely an observation. "Yeah, yesterday was a killer."

"And you're flying again today?"

Fishing my cell phone from the nightstand, I answer, "Another red eye, I'm afraid."

He doesn't respond, probably because this is a conversation we've already had.

"Nina is picking Sophie up from practice."

He tosses a towel in my direction. "And Hayley?"

Pretending not to have heard him, I stare at my screen. One less lie I'll have to tell with a straight face. Scanning my email for the day's itinerary, I tap on a subject line that reads: *Dan and Jackie–Anniversary Dinner.* The email contains three paragraphs of text. Attached are several photos of a dinner party.

DEAR ONES,

Thank you for coming out to share our anniversary. It was a magical night filled with all the people we love. What a blessing it was.

Just a reminder, we're hosting game night next Wednesday. Should start around 7:30 and end around 9:15 or so. Hope to see you there! <3

Love to you all —

Jackie

P.S. Please update your contact list with Dan's new email: Dantheman22407@ymail.com

IGNORING THE WORDS, I EXTRACT THE NUMBERS AND SYMBOLS which make up the password that enables me to access compressed data stored in the tedious photos. Back when I first learned how this worked, I thought it was a little risky, sending so much information in an email anyone could read. Covert communication is key, I was told. They could encrypt the messages, but even if they were unbreakable, they'd draw attention. It made sense. No one gives a crap about other people's vacation photos, at least not to the extent to look too deeply into them.

"Charlotte?" Michael calls from the bathroom. "Have you gone back to sleep?"

"No. Just making a grocery list."

"I asked about Hayley."

"Oh—" I scroll through another email before filing it away in a folder to be read later. "I thought you were picking her up."

"Me?"

I don't answer. Sometimes it is best to let people come to their own conclusions. Eventually, the shower turns on.

I ease out of bed, roll my neck, and make a beeline for the closet in search of something sufficient enough to hide my injuries.

Michael peeks his head around the bathroom door. I've forgotten. He doesn't like to argue on days I fly. "I'll see if I can cut out early," he says. "If not, I'll ring the Terrys."

I hear his words. But they don't register. My mind has already flung itself far into the future, into the data, to the job I have to do. Carpool is the least of my concerns. I have a murder to plan.

CHAPTER THREE

Charlotte

As I slap mayonnaise between two slices of bread, I run through it in my mind. Calling my shot, I watch it play out, making sure to envision the outcome I want, just as athletes do before a big match. Henry taught me this. Murder is mostly a mental game.

This is a theory I'll be forced to put to the test today, considering that my body aches in unfamiliar places and I'm slightly delirious. I just hope Henry's right. I really need today to be cut and dry.

My husband notices. I know because he's commented— not once, but twice—that I've over-extended myself this month making too many bids, which he rarely does.

We need the money. At least that's what I told him. College and retirement always come faster than you think, I said, knowing he couldn't argue with me on that.

That's not to say I don't see his point. I'm not fond of back to back trips, either. They don't give me much time to think, and it's the build-up I miss most when things move this quickly. How lovely it is to have segments of time set aside, just to imagine, to daydream, and maybe even to grocery shop. Those stolen moments that make a job well done that much sweeter.

It's important to take them when you can. I'm taking one now, as I slice deeply into the turkey sandwich, making a perfect diagonal cut. I imagine the elongated throat of my mark, opening slowly, offering blood, giving life over to death, and suddenly I feel a deep sense of peace. It occurs to me that I'm exactly where I'm supposed to be, doing exactly what I'm supposed to be doing.

It's a beautiful moment, until my youngest daughter enters the kitchen and begins slinging things around, rendering any sort of substantial thought nearly impossible. "Have you seen my math homework?"

I glance up from my sandwich artistry, a hint of warning in my eyes. At thirteen, she is as petulant as they come, alternating between thinking she is an adult and acting like a child. "Nope."

She slams her fist into the granite. "I left it right here!" Her eyes meet mine. I offer a tight smile noticing how much she looks like me at that age, with subtle hints of her father thrown in. "I put it here," she screeches, stabbing her finger at the countertop. "Right here."

"I doubt it grew legs," I say, knowing how it will land. Someday all that pent-up anger will serve her well. But not today, so I motion toward the door. "Out of my kitchen. I have to finish lunches. And I have a flight to catch."

As I watch Hayley stomp off, Michael wanders in, his gazed fixed on the Josie Natori silk caftan I threw on while he was in the shower. A gift from Henry. "What's her deal?"

"Poor organizational skills."

"Let me guess...her homework?" He walks over, pausing in the doorway and shouts after her, "Check the dining room!"

Eventually, Sophie saunters in, her skirt beyond several inches too short. It's miles in the wrong direction, hovering just below the crease where her behind meets her upper thigh. I palm the knife, gripping it so tight my fingers go numb. I watch Michael take note. Disapproval and something else—worry, I think—passes over his face. It's not her fault entirely. She's testing her limits, but only to a degree. It doesn't help her cause that she's all arms and legs, just like her father. At fifteen, the rest of her hasn't grown into them yet, which makes it awkward watching her lurch herself from one place to the next, never seeming sure of exactly who or where she is.

She makes a beeline for the fridge. "Who's picking me up today?"

"Nina."

I notice a subtle shift in her features. A faint smile. Sophie's more controlled than her sister, more like me in that regard. She doesn't wear her emotions on her sleeve, which means I have to watch closely. "I can just get a ride with Toby."

"Your mother has already arranged for you to ride home with Nina," Michael tells her, his tone leaving no room for rebuttal. He often forgets his daughters aren't little girls anymore, but this morning it seems he remembers. "And that outfit isn't going to pass dress code."

Sophie buries her head in the refrigerator, but I feel the eye roll from across the room. "Whatever."

"I can't afford to get a call from the school, Soph—I'm in meetings all day and your mother is flying."

"Fine!" she hisses, slamming the refrigerator door closed. "I'll change."

I'm just about to reprimand her for yelling when Michael asks where I'm flying to, catching me off guard. He rarely asks anymore, and I rarely offer more information than I have to.

"Oh," I say, screwing the lid on the mayonnaise. "Um...Florida, I think."

His bottom lip juts out. "Florida doesn't sound half bad."

25

My eyes meet his. "Oh yeah? When's the last time you've been there?"

When he raises his brow, I know it's a point well made.

It's blissfully quiet for a moment, until Hayley storms in brandishing her phone. "This thing sucks."

Michael shrugs.

"It's dead. Again!"

"You have to charge it," Sophie scoffs. "But you probably forgot that too."

"I did...*jerk.*" I watch Hayley as she sits down on a barstool and sulks. "It had like...twenty percent battery!"

When no one responds to her, she tries harder to get the attention she is after. "I keep telling you guys. I need a new one."

"What you need," I tell her, "is a job."

"All right," Michael cuts in, sensing WWIII coming on. "Let's go." He swoops around the counter and leans in for a peck on my cheek. "Everybody out the door."

"How am I supposed to get a job? I'm just a kid," Hayley says shoving her books in her bag, but looking at her now, we both know it isn't true.

Michael gives me the once-over. "You'll be back tonight?" I watch as he stuffs his keys and his phone into his pocket. There's something he's not saying.

My stomach seizes. "That's the plan."

He makes the universal *whew* sign, placing his hand to his forehead. Eventually, he leans in for another peck. "Good," he says. "Because I couldn't do this without you."

"Nor I you."

If there's something he'd wanted to say, he's changed his mind. He's all smiles as he heads out the door. Me too, because it's finally quiet, and I can think about murder.

CHAPTER FOUR

Charlotte

You blink and you're making your descent into Dulles. Blink again and you're on the runway at McCarren. Blink three times and you're landing at Teterboro. You takeoff at Van Nuys, land at Love Field. Look up and you're taxiing at Hobby. That's life. Always up in the air. That's certainly how I feel now, trying to get out the door, realizing I forgot to switch the laundry over, and I'm destined to head to the airport in a damp uniform. It's also where I first encountered Henry Noble. Henry, with his sleepy eyes and stoic demeanor. I was just back from maternity leave—a prolonged leave, but I was back nonetheless. It's hard to believe that was almost fifteen years ago now—that is, unless I look in the mirror, at which point it's suddenly evident. There's little left of the girl I was back then.

In fact, almost nothing at all.

I hadn't planned to return to work as a flight attendant after Sophie was born. At least, not until the recession hit, and the project list at Michael's architecture firm went from having a waitlist to drying up completely. I'd thought I might try my hand at writing a novel, or a screenplay, something frivolous. In the end, there was no sense in having two unemployed parents, and so back to the skies I went.

The silver lining was the fact that I'd been offered a sweet little gig with a private charter company. This meant no more commercial flights. More importantly, the charter company paid better. I wouldn't have to make as many bids. I wouldn't have to spend so much time away.

I had been back at work for about three weeks when I met Henry on a flight from Bergstrom to Teterboro. We had been transporting a dignitary, I think. Or something of the sort. It's odd to me that this is the aspect of the job that interests most people. I've never really cared. Not even back then. A trip is a trip is a trip. Which is to say, pretty much, they're all the same.

It wasn't until our third flight together that I really got the chance to know Henry. We boarded a big plane that day—the more important the passenger, the bigger the jet—but that much probably goes without saying. The crew consisted of the pilot, copilot, and two cabin attendants: Henry and me.

We were in charge of a single passenger, a graying, dark-skinned man with overbearing features and impeccable style. Italian, if I had to guess. This meant there wasn't a lot to do on the first leg of the flight. Even though I didn't know much about Henry, I had surmised he wasn't one for small talk, which I found to be a relief. God knows there is enough of that embedded in the job.

I remember feeling glad I'd thought to bring along a book. I've heard it said that nothing is more important than an unread library. I believe it. I counted the minutes until we reached cruising altitude and I could slide that true crime novel from my bag and immerse myself.

Later, as I read, I felt Henry's eyes on me, more curious than anything. Still, a decision was made. If he interrupted my reading, not only could we not be cordial any longer, I knew I'd spend the rest of the flight plotting his demise.

We were mid-flight, and I was somewhere around page 180 when Henry stood from his seat and made his way up the cabin. Back then I was still fairly green when it came to being a waitress in the sky on private flights, and I recall thinking there must have been something I'd missed. Although Henry and I had agreed to work in shifts, and the first leg was his, there was something in his gait that struck me as odd.

My eyes followed his feet.

By the time they stopped moving, I could hear what that thing was. A slight gurgling sound—heavy coughing, followed by unmistakable chest rattling. I craned my neck, trying to get a better look. With Henry's torso blocking the view, ultimately I was forced to stand and make my way up the aisle, where Henry stood looming over our passenger. When I reached him, Henry's head was slightly cocked. His hands rested on his hips. The Italian appeared to be trying to speak while alternately gripping his throat and pleading with his hands. His face was a perfect cherry red, making it clear what the problem was. Still, Henry peered down at him as though perplexed. I remember thinking it was one of the strangest and most beautiful things I'd ever seen.

I asked Henry what he was doing as I simultaneously shoved him aside. "He's choking," I said. "We're trained for this."

"Precisely," he answered, one corner of his lip turned upward. Henry was not then, and still isn't now, the smiling kind.

I shook my head and went in for the kill, wrapping my arms around the Italian. Pressing my stomach to his back, I gave the Heimlich my best shot. It was a struggle. The man was larger than

I'd anticipated, and I found it difficult to get my arms around him.
"Henry!"

"Let it be," Henry said.

"It's not working," I grunted. "I can't—"

He watched me, wordless, as the Italian's face turned an indigo blue.

"Work with me," I begged the passenger, reaching, heaving, praying for a bit of give but finding nothing of the sort. He flailed about haplessly, like a fish out of water, while also purring like a cat, which sounds funny, but that's the sensation I felt with my body pressed against his. A white foamy substance dribbled from his mouth onto my wrist. He lurched forward, fighting me, as he struggled for air. It was impossible to dislodge whatever was blocking his airway if he refused to let me get my arms around him. Nonetheless, the milky foam kept falling from his lips. My arms were coated in it. It smelled like old cheese, and it was warm—the kind of thing you don't forget. Like a smile out of Henry, if you're ever lucky enough to squeeze one out.

"Probably a fish bone," Henry noted, nodding at the man's half-eaten lunch. Antipasti, lake trout, fresh figs, and Vernaccia wine. Not exactly the kind of food you get flying commercial.

"Are you going to help?" I said to Henry, as I stuck two fingers down the man's throat, swabbing side to side. "Or should I summon the pilot?"

"It won't be long now," he answered, glancing at his watch. A vintage Rolex—I noticed it the first time we met. Over the last few weeks, it had become more and more apparent that not only did Henry have a watch fetish, he had quite the collection. "Just hold on."

I gave him a sideways look. At first glance, Henry had appeared ordinary enough. Hardworking, intelligent, and possibly gay, given his quietly expensive taste. In his late twenties, I presumed, with the kind of face you instantly forget. But there was something more, an unblinking watchfulness about him, one that no doubt made him good at the job that was not so ordinary.

Henry glanced at his watch again.

I relaxed my arms, and the Italian slumped forward.

"This is very unfortunate," Henry said, checking the man's pulse. "He's breathing. Faintly."

"What the fuck—" My mouth hung open, only closing long enough to suck in air, which eventually allowed me to complete my question. "What are we going to do?"

Henry's brow furrowed momentarily and then his eyes widened in surprise. "Damn."

"What?"

"It wasn't a fish bone."

I frowned. I didn't follow.

"You put the peanut glaze on his salad, didn't you?"

"I don't know." I shrugged. "Maybe."

Henry watched me for a second, taking note of my condition, of the breathlessness, of my incessant panting. He commented that I could use some fitness training. Considering the day I was having, I didn't entirely disagree. He waited for a response before realizing I wasn't going to offer one. Eventually, he made a clucking sound with his tongue. "Says on this profile he's allergic to nuts."

I felt everything drain out of me at once. This situation was going to require a lot of paperwork, and if I were really and truly unlucky, possibly jail time. Definitely a lengthy court case when the charter company was sued. No doubt I'd have to testify, and I hate an audience. "Fuck."

"Missed that, huh?"

My throat was too dry for me to speak. Another shrug was all I could offer.

"You managed to read a novel, but not his profile?"

I cocked one eyebrow. I imagined myself leaning forward and, despite my lack of fitness, snapping Henry's neck. It wouldn't save my job, but it might make me feel better about the impending loss of it.

Henry considered me carefully. "Okay," he said, handing over the salad plate. "Here's what we're going to do." He scanned the cabin and motioned toward the plate in my hand. "Take that and get rid of the evidence."

I nodded, feeling relieved he was so good at making himself useful. The last thing I needed was more blood on my hands.

"In a few minutes," he told me with a heavy sigh, "I'll alert the pilot that we need to make an emergency landing."

"He'll be dead by then."

"Likely, yes." There was a hint of impatience in his reply.

"What are we going to say?"

"The truth," Henry replied. "That he choked."

I told him I didn't understand, even though I kind of did.

"In time you will."

I felt pins and needles in my stomach. "Shouldn't we just tell the actual truth?"

"What's the point? He's going to die either way."

"But it's my fault."

"Hardly," Henry scoffed. "He had a weakness. You were just doing your job."

I narrowed my eyes, trying to comprehend what he was saying and, more importantly, what he wasn't.

"It's just a white lie," Henry said with a shrug. "A simple omission."

"A simple omission," I repeated, feeling slightly calmer.

Henry walked over to where I stood. When he spoke, he did so slowly and calmly, like he was speaking to a child. "I think this is something you could be really good at."

"I don't understand." I shook my head. "Why didn't you help? And why are you covering for me?"

Later Henry would explain everything. Right then, he simply

sighed. "The slump of your shoulders tells me you can't afford to lose your job."

I straightened my back, but he wasn't wrong. Henry leaned down and removed the man's watch from his wrist. He didn't smile when he held it up, but there was a gleam in his eye that was unmistakable. "It's a Bvlgari."

CHAPTER FIVE

Charlotte

I t's early afternoon in Fort Lauderdale, the bright winter sun high in the sky. I am seated at an outside table at Estero, a private, members-only club. Hints of wisteria fill the moist air. Even in winter, the club's flower garden is on full display, if you're into that sort of thing—but that's not why I came.

It's warm out, far warmer than Texas, and sweat beads at my temples where the auburn wig meets my skin. My hand rests lightly on the stem of my glass. I feel a pleasing exhaustion as I raise it to my lips.

The cool liquid goes down smoothly. It's almost enough to take the edge off. My senses are heightened, as they always are when it comes to work.

Glancing at the time, I know I don't have long to accomplish what I've come for. It's a short layover, but still, I can't rush this.

In endeavors where lives are on the line, I remind myself it's important to wait, to be noticed when the time is right, like the flowers. Taking another slow sip of my vodka martini, I discreetly survey my surroundings. It's crowded for midweek. Most of the other tables are occupied, but I only have eyes for one.

The conversation there has halted.

The couple seated at the adjacent table—where things seem to have stalled and where my attention is drawn—look bored. He's in his sixties and has a moneyed, careless way about him. His companion is thirty-five. Maybe. Whatever her age, she's exquisite, with a feline quality and jagged features to match. They aren't married, at least not to each other. It's possible they're colleagues. Distant cousins, maybe. Lovers is where I'd place my money, if we were betting.

Several minutes go by, and I decide, definitely not cousins. Although I am in Florida, so you never know. Nevertheless, I have my doubts. There's a certain tension between them, palpable chemistry that's anything but familial.

Catching my eye, the man raises his glass of red, tilting it in my direction. He murmurs to his companion, who then shifts, pinning me with an icy stare. "Care to join us?"

Her offer is every bit as much a challenge as it is an invitation, and lucky for us both, it's one I've been waiting for. I run my eyes over the length of her, a cool breeze rustling the scented air.

"No obligations," the man says, his upbeat tone at odds with his downturned mouth. "Just an invitation."

His offer is precisely the kind I'd hoped for, which is why I scoot from my table, grab my glass, and resettle myself in a chair between them. My eyes dart back and forth toward the entrance. They burn, both from sleepiness and from irritation of the contacts I use to conceal my natural eye color. "I'm waiting on a colleague," I confess. "But she must have gotten held up."

"I'm Richard." He offers his hand, then with a swift sweep of his head, he says, "And this is Janine."

You don't say. "Olivia."

Once introductions have been made, the conversation unfolds

easily. I learn Richard is an inventor (retired) and Janine a model (also retired). They are not colleagues nor do they offer the vibe of being lovers upon closer inspection. Nevertheless, there are erotic undertones in their involvement, evident in the way they seem pleased to have drawn me in.

"So, tell me, Olivia," Janine smiles. "What are you into?"

"Real estate, mostly," I answer, my face fresh and hungry. Overly eager. *I'm sorry I killed your father. What was he like? Did he tell you about me? Is this my fault? Do you have daddy issues?* This is more along the lines of the type of Q&A I came for, but of course, that's not what I say. "For the most part, I work with buyers." I pause just long enough to sip my drink. Dropping my chin, I raise my gaze, allowing my mouth to linger on the rim. "But on occasion, sellers too."

It takes a second, given the way the information is delivered, but inevitably their eyes glaze over. The moment a person thinks you're trying to sell them, is the moment the conversation is over.

I can, if necessary, drone on endlessly about real estate, but they don't care to know. Instead, I describe my recent trip to Africa, a hunting expedition. I've never actually been to Africa, but I can picture the trip down to the terrible khaki, the necessity of understanding the bell curve, and the weaponry involved in killing big game. None of which interests them in the least, and that is the point.

My lies flow as effortlessly as the drinks. It's a perfect story, and deception always offers a pleasant rush. My panties would be wet, if I were wearing any.

"It's such a pleasure to have met you," Richard tells me, his voice lower than before. "You resemble someone I used to know."

"Yes," his companion purrs. "We love your eyes, and that *dress* —and *my God*, Richard, have you seen those heels?"

He has. I know, because not only have I not spared any expense, I've positioned myself just so. Laughing the woman off, I imagine her friend moving his hands deftly and possessively over my body. Undoubtedly, my thoughts are reflected in my eyes. He's not my type, but it helps to keep the feelings real, and to keep the feelings real, it helps to go there. Imagination is everything.

It's obvious in the way he glares back at me. He views me, I can tell, as something to own, a nice collectible to stick on a shelf and admire when it suits him. He believes he is in control. Most men do.

I look away, the flush of my cheeks evident.

"Is that so hard to imagine?" Janine asks. "That we find you stunning?"

"No," I reply, somewhat harshly. "It isn't."

She looks surprised. It's not the first time she has registered something may be off. But she isn't certain and she doesn't want to disappoint her friend, so when she starts to speak, she thinks better of it, pressing her lips together instead. They're familiar, in a certain kind of way. I picture myself reaching out and running my finger over them, fake as they may be. I suppose it doesn't matter, if they taste the same. There's a part of me that desperately wants to find out.

My phone chimes. Fishing it out of my clutch, I see it instantly. The one word text: BOUNCE.

Apologizing to my new friends, I tell them I've gotten the location of the meeting wrong, and without another word, I am in a town car bound for the airport.

CHAPTER SIX

Charlotte

The town car weaves in and out of rush hour traffic. My phone estimates the drive back to the airport will take all of twenty minutes, but looking out the window, I'm not so sure. I should feel relief at the delay, but I don't. I feel nothing.

My forehead falls against the cool glass as I arrange the pieces of the puzzle in my mind. There are endless questions that can be asked, answers that can always be found.

I don't know why Henry followed me; I only know that the past is never through with us.

He taught me that, way back when. Back when Sophie was a baby, and long before Hayley had ever been thought of. Back when I objected to the idea that I would be good at this gig. *You have to be kidding*, I'd said to him. It just sounds so cliché. *Like a joke.*

I laughed him off, even as they carried the Italian off the plane in a body bag. Mostly because a part of me thought it was a joke.

It seemed I'd earned myself a starring role on a TV show where any minute someone was going to jump out and yell *gotcha!* But then I realized, who would do such a thing? I don't have any friends, or at least I didn't at the time, and Michael's sense of humor is far too dry to pull that kind of prank, nor does he care about such trivial matters.

"Don't we have to talk to the police?" I asked. "Write a report?"

This time it was Henry's turn to laugh. "Why would we? There's no record of him having been on this plane."

"I see."

"I've been watching you," Henry said with conviction. It was the first time I considered that he might actually be serious.

"You've only known me a few weeks."

"That's what you think."

"What does that mean?" *Who are you?*

"You've been on our radar."

"You're going to have to speak English. Because I don't understand."

"We make it a point to look for people like you."

"You have a thing for new moms?" I said flippantly, instantly regretting it. It was the first time since Sophie's birth, maybe ever, that I had the sensation of what it might be like to have to— to *want* to—protect someone else.

"That is unfortunate, the child," Henry answered solemnly. "But also leverage."

He was right. I understood then. He knew more than I thought.

"You and I," he said, motioning between us. "We come from vastly different backgrounds, I know. But the common denominators are a keen eye when it comes to observing human nature and a conviction that justice is rarely served in a way that makes a difference to the wronged."

"Oh good," I remarked. "A philosopher."

"Call it what you want. It's what I've learned from observing you."

"Observations can be wrong."

"Maybe. But I recognize the look in your eye. And I know what it means."

"What's that?"

"Well...let's see. Age twenty-one. Married. One child. Homeowner. Average debt—at least by American standards. Unemployed husband. Marginally desperate."

"Any street corner palm reader worth their salt could have come up with that."

His eyes shifted downward. "Your mother cut out on you early. You hate weak people. Your dad was a cop. And you share his penchant for seeing justice served."

"Justice—" I said, thinking he had no idea what he was talking about. "That's interesting. Justice for who?"

Henry laughed knowingly. "No rush. We'll get to that."

"I'm sure of it." I plopped down into a seat on the aisle.

"Anyway, point is," he said, taking the seat adjacent to mine. "You have talent. You can shoot. And you spent twelve years in martial arts."

"More like after school care."

"You really shouldn't downplay your skillset, Charlotte. It goes against your diagnosis."

"I don't have a diagnosis."

"Perhaps not," he replied, his voice low. He glanced out the window, his eyes focused on the tarmac. "But you've killed before. As a matter of fact, you killed your college sweetheart a few years ago, although that wasn't the last time, was it?" Before I could respond he looked back at me. "And the most notable thing about it is you didn't get caught."

My pulse quickened. Maybe it was nerves. Maybe it just felt good that someone else knew.

"Tell me," he said. "What did you feel when you did it?"

I stared at him for a long time.

Eventually, his expression softened. "Hypothetically speaking, of course?"

"I suppose at the time I felt satisfied."

"And now?"

"Now, nothing."

Henry smiled. Something I had not seen from him, not before and I don't think since. I almost smiled too. Just saying the words brought great pleasure. Like a release, only not just any release. Like a pressure value, tightly screwed on, had suddenly just blown wide open.

His eyes lit up. "The world needs more people like you."

"I don't know about that," I told him. No one had ever said anything like that to me, I realized.

"You don't know what you don't know, Charlotte."

"Clearly."

"Men and women—people like us, who are different, who lack a conscience, who possess an absence of the ability to feel guilt— it's a great equalizer on this planet. A necessity, honestly."

"What is it you want from me?"

Dangling the proverbial carrot over my head, he went on to explain that he knew what I had done and was prepared to destroy me with his knowledge, essentially taking my family down with me, separating me from my daughter, just as my mother had been taken away. Then a funny thing happened. I was surprised to find I didn't hate him for it. It was as though my whole life finally made sense, as though everything had led me to that moment.

CHAPTER SEVEN

Charlotte

The first time I killed a man, I was nineteen and a sophomore in college. Henry was wrong in his assumption that he was my college sweetheart, but he was close. We had slept together.

His name was Brad, and he was my roommate's boyfriend. I liked him well enough. Not enough for a second date, but enough that if she had friends over, and he was in the mix, I'd share a drink or two with them.

When she asked if I minded if she dated him, I lied and told her I kind of did. Not because I cared. But because he wasn't her type.

Megan was sweet and full of life. Brad was sadistic and harbored a secret hatred for women that, like most sociopaths, he managed to push way down deep. In other words, they were perfect for each other.

Megan was easy prey for a monster like him.

Brad was a perfect disaster for her and her idyllic worldview.

One night just after the start of the second semester, this became more apparent, when Megan called me from Brad's fraternity house asking for a ride. I had been busy studying and wasn't particularly in the mood for a rescue mission. It wasn't like I hadn't warned her.

Everyone at the party was well past the legal limit. She said I was her only hope. It was cold, and she didn't want to walk. I mentioned that my car didn't have heat and suggested a cab, but then she started crying and brought up that she'd covered the electric bill the month prior, when my waitressing job was slow.

I was between a rock and a hard place, and it only went downhill from there. The rest was drunk girl blubbering, and I couldn't make out exactly what she was saying except that she and Brad had had a fight.

When I arrived, Megan wasn't waiting on the curb like she'd promised. Five minutes became fifteen. A quarter of an hour bled into a half hour. I didn't have heat in my car, nor enough gas to keep the engine running, so I was forced to either leave her and take the chance of getting another call, or go in after her.

I should have realized then that the evening wasn't going to end well. Maybe I was bored, or lonely, or maybe I was pissed and looking for a challenge. Maybe it was all of those things.

But I got out of the car. Then I stayed. I eventually found Megan in the back chatting up a group of girls I didn't know. I never have been one for small talk or superficiality, and I wasn't at school to make friends. She told me she'd only be a minute. I should have left then. The same guilt that should have led me home instead led me to the keg.

My father was picking up extra shifts to cover my living expenses and tuition, moonlighting at concerts and sporting events, putting up with the exact kind of drunk crowd I was now mingling with.

I should have been back at my dorm studying, trying to graduate early, trying to save my dad some money. But I wasn't.

"Excuse me," a thick voice said from behind me. "I can't get by."

When I turned around, that thing they say happens, happened. Deep in the pit of my stomach, something took hold and refused to let go. He didn't look like a student, but by then I'd had several drinks, and I wasn't much of a drinker.

I moved aside to let him pass.

"Have we met?" he asked.

I shook my head and tried not to look him in the eye. I wasn't there to meet anyone, and he looked like precisely the kind of trouble I was trying to avoid. He looked like there would be three kids and a minivan in my future.

"Are you sure?"

I shrugged.

"You're Erin's friend?"

Sipping my beer, I moved out of the narrow hall and into the living area, thinking I might suffocate. When I made it to the sofa, which was covered in happy drunks, he met me shoulder to shoulder.

"Erin—have you seen her?"

I had no idea who he was talking about. I motioned toward the stairs and glanced up toward the second floor. "Maybe check up there?"

"I have," he said, clearly annoyed. "Twice."

Scanning the room, I searched for a way out. "Sorry, I just got here."

He ran his fingers through his hair. "She called me for a ride but I can't find her anywhere…I might not even be at the right house, for fuck's sake. She's drunk and the music was loud. I think I got the wrong address." He glanced at the drink in my hand. "Could be any house on this street."

"Good luck." I started walking away. "I need to find my friend."

"Sisters," he said with a scoff, following close behind. "Do you have one?"

"No."

He stuck his hand out. "I'm Michael, by the way."

I asked if he wanted to take a shot. I wasn't in the mood for conversation. Something about his fingers made me realize I just wanted to fuck.

"Will it get me your name?"

"Maybe."

"Then *maybe* I do."

I took his hand and led him toward the kitchen, where Jell-O shots were lined up on the counter. Eyeballing the spread, he said, "I think I'm a bit too old for this."

I handed him a small plastic cup and took one for myself. "My grandma eats Jell-O. Is she too old?"

He smiled and then slurped it down like an oyster on the half shell. I watched the way his throat moved as he swallowed and felt a chill down my spine. Then I placed the plastic to my lips and followed suit. "Olivia," I said after the third round.

"Olivia," he repeated, surprised or suspicious or both. He leaned forward and pressed his thumb to my lip. When he pulled it away, he held it up. A bit of Jell-O was stuck to the tip. He popped it in his mouth and sucked the tip. "You wanna get out of here?" he asked glancing around the kitchen. He leaned in and lowered his voice even though the music was loud. The way he smelled made me weak in the knees. I mentally calculated how long it had been since I'd gotten laid. "I'm sorry," he added. "This isn't exactly my scene."

I grabbed a handful of Jell-O shots, conveniently lidded, and shoved them in the pocket of my coat. With only a slight nod, he motioned toward the door. "What about your sister?"

He smiled. "I don't have a sister," he said, and I think I fell a little in love.

His car wasn't a clunker like mine. When he opened the door for me, I thought about how low the bar had been set for the other men in my life, and how I needed to keep it that way. After he'd settled into the driver's seat, he turned to me and raised his brow. "Where to?"

I pressed my lips to one another and gave him the satisfaction of pretending to think it over. "Your place?"

His apartment was not like the apartments of other boys. There weren't posters on the wall or bongs littering the table. It didn't smell like leftover food. Maybe it was because he was older, but I got the sense that he was different. I was worried he might not want to fuck.

But then he put on a record, Nat King Cole, something I'd never heard before. I don't think anyone in our generation had, and I told him as much. He laughed, a full head back, throaty kind of laugh. "It sort of grows on you."

Does it now? I smiled, but I don't remember doing much talking that night. He did enough for the both of us. He asked me to dance, and he told me lame jokes. He told me what he did for a living and about where he grew up. Later, after we'd finally fucked, as he drifted off to sleep, he whispered that I should be careful. I was the kind of person he could easily fall in love with.

Even though the sex was actually pretty good, despite a slight vanilla touch, I knew then it would be the last time I saw him.

I laid there staring at the ceiling, wondering how long I had to wait before waking him from sleep to ask for a ride home. Finally, my pager went off. It was Megan, and it read 9-1-1, followed by the address of the fraternity house. I decided a clean break would be easier. It would be better that way. No awkward explanations, no half-hearted promises of seeing each other again. Quietly, I climbed out of bed, dressed, and walked the three miles it took to get back to the fraternity.

It was just after 3:00 a.m. when I arrived. The party was still in full swing, albeit the crowd a little thinner, a little more subdued. I found Megan in the bathroom with a bloody nose and black eye, naked from the waist down, semi-conscious.

"Megan—" I shook her hard. "What the fuck?"

She mumbled my name. Maybe she said *why'd you leave?* Maybe she begged me to stay. Her words were jumbled and unclear. As I wrapped her in a towel, I noticed the blood smeared between her thighs.

"Megan," I hissed, searching for her clothes, for something to cover her with. "Megan—who did this?"

She mumbled inaudibly.

I took off my jacket and covered her legs. I started to tie it around her waist. "Where are your pants? Did Brad do this?"

"We had a fight," she slurred. "I told you."

I didn't kill Bradley Simmons that night. I wish I had. He raped and beat Megan two more times. Each time she promised—she *swore*—she'd end things. Each time she didn't.

After the third time, the last time, the time he broke her arm, I made sure I was in attendance at his next frat party. I made sure he drank more than usual and that Megan did as well. She should have known, they both should have, that alcohol and painkillers don't mix.

Once Brad had passed out, I drove her home and tucked her safely into bed. Then I drove back to the fraternity house, entered through the back door, and found him in his room. I slipped my hands around his throat, feeling the weight of his head in my hands, how effortlessly his neck held it up. I thought about snapping it. Like a twig. I imagined myself, choking the life out of him just as he was doing to Megan.

But I knew that was risky.

I knew I'd leave a mark. Evidence. So instead, I placed a pillow over his face and sat on it, bearing down with the entirety of my being. He struggled, but only a little. The music was loud, the beat thumping in time with his movement. It was pure art, the give and take between us, a wonderful dance as his whole world stopped. It was too bad he couldn't even hold out the entire song.

CHAPTER EIGHT

Charlotte

"I'm sorry," I said to my father. "I don't have a choice." I'd just turned twenty and was, in essence, a full-blown adult. But in that moment, standing there in front of his recliner, I'd never felt more like a child. A girl, who, in four short months, was going to have one of her own.

"We always have a choice."

Shaking my head slowly, I looked away, hoping it might stop my chin from quivering. "It's too late to have an abortion."

My father didn't respond. When I glanced back at him, he didn't look me in the eye.

"He changed his mind. He isn't going to leave his wife."

"I tried to tell you Char—they never do."

"I'm sorry," I said again, and it was the truth. I hated to disappoint him. I'd been on a roll lately, and this, while surely the biggest, was just one more in a long succession of letdowns.

"First the incident at school," he said, reading my mind, "and now this."

"I wasn't learning anything I didn't already know anyway."

"Clearly," he answered, bitterly. My father had saved every penny he could, a single parent, on a cop's salary, to send me to college and the semester before, after the incident with Brad, I'd dropped out. My father reminded me of his sacrifice often.

I'd planned to finish school. I just found the whole thing so distracting, so ripe with possibilities. The truth is, I'd never felt more complete, more whole, than I did after I killed Bradley Simmons. Nothing, not even sex, had ever brought me that much satisfaction. This lasted for days, the high, the fullness of it. Even as Megan cried day in and day out, even hugging Brad's mother at his funeral, throwing dirt on his casket, I'd never felt more alive. I replayed the act over and over for days. It took about two weeks for the high to wear off.

When it did, I knew that I had to find that feeling again.

I just had to pick my next victim. But what could make me feel as strongly as Bradley had? I didn't yet know.

And then, over drinks with Megan weeks afterward, I let something slip. I told her I was glad he was dead. I was glad he couldn't hurt her anymore. Maybe it was the way I said it, but something for her seemed to click. "You drugged me," she said, her voice edged with wariness. "That night. The night that Brad died."

I didn't deny it. I simply put my switchblade to her throat and asked her to write a note. Megan was found hanging from our doorjamb the following day. She'd been so distraught after her boyfriend's death. No one seemed all that surprised.

After that, I grew bored with school. Decided I had to get out of that town where nothing ever happened. I needed to see the world. I applied for a job as a flight attendant and was shocked when three weeks later I got the call.

"I'm going back to waitressing," I told my father. "But after...I plan to fly again."

"Things never quite work out the way you think they will, Charlotte."

I knew what he meant. Or at least I thought I did. I hadn't been flying long, just about three months, when I met Dan, a captain on a crew I flew with regularly.

It was the first job I didn't hate. It helped that I was out of Dad's hair, and I was doing something he could be proud of—not college-level proud, but proud nonetheless. Then I met Dan. And then, just like with school, everything changed.

What had started as a one-night stand quickly grew into a fling and then into an unwanted and unexpected pregnancy.

I might have been young, but I wasn't all together stupid. I knew Dan didn't want another child. His own children were nearly grown, not so far from my age. So I told him not to worry and scheduled the abortion for a random Tuesday on a sunny day in May.

I showed up for my appointment and was surprised to find the clinic was roped off. Cop cars and ambulances lined the block. From across the street a familiar voice called my name. It was my father's. He asked what I was doing there.

Looking for you, I'd said. Something we both knew was a lie.

You shouldn't be here, he told me. Just an hour earlier, he explained, a gunman had entered the clinic and shot and killed eleven people.

When I called Dan to tell him, he told me it would be fine. We'd think of something. Over the coming weeks, I couldn't bring myself to make another appointment. I didn't really want to have to face my dad. More than anything, I was probably afraid.

Eventually, Dan promised me he'd tell his wife. He said she'd leave him, or vice versa, that we would be together, that everything would be fine. But of course it was all a lie. He was friendly enough when I told him I couldn't go through with the abortion, but as the weeks went by and I began to show, he began to distance himself.

"I won't bother you with any of it," I promised my dad. "I just need to know I have a place to stay until she is born."

His eyes met mine. "This is your home. You know that."

Glancing at my father in his La-Z-Boy, I felt exactly as I had as a child, when I'd made a mess, or broken something, or said the wrong thing, or watched the TV with the volume too high. In those days, before she left for good, my mother would rage and yell and slam the front door, leaving my father and me alone. He would call me over to him, set me on his lap, and tell me one of his police stories. One of the good ones, with the happy endings. Afterward, he would smooth my hair and say, "Go clean your room," or "When she comes back, make sure you say you're sorry," and most often, "Just fix it."

But this time he did not call me into his lap, and he did not smooth my hair. He did not tell me to fix it. He sat and stared at the muted TV, his eyes fixed, his jaw set.

"I'm sorry," I said again, and just briefly which didn't happen often, I wished my mother were there. I would have given anything for shouting and slamming doors over the deafening silence.

"I can't believe you'd give away your own child," he said, and then he turned the TV up as loud as he could.

CHAPTER NINE

Charlotte

"What were you thinking?" Henry demands to know the second I step foot on the plane. I have to give credit where credit is due—Henry asks really good questions.

The meeting at Estero was risky. Janine and Richard were not the reason I was in Florida. I considered the risk. I knew there was the chance of ruining things before they had ever gotten off the ground. I knew all of this before we ever landed. I just didn't think any of it was probable. Plus, I was thinking about other things.

I was thinking about my appearance, wondering if it would be enough to draw him in. I was thinking about how to handle it if I did, understanding I had to be careful.

I was thinking about the consequence if I wasn't.

This seems like a lot to explain, so when Henry repeats the question again, I simply say, "I'm not sure what you mean."

Henry's face darkens, as quickly as a cloud moving in front of the sun. "Your lunch date."

"That's not what I'd call a date."

"Yeah...well—" He nods at my dress. "I beg to differ."

I smile. I can't help myself. "You like it?" I ask, striking a bit of a pose. I knew he would. "It's Zuhair Mur—"

"He had eyes on him, Liv."

"I know." Turning away, I give the overhead bin an irritable shake. Lies require noise and misdirection. Silence is the best way to draw the truth to the surface, which is why I leave it at that.

"If you knew...then what in the hell were you doing?"

I turn and smile. "Having fun."

"My God—I don't know what the fuck I'm supposed to say to that."

I don't know either. I could tell him he shouldn't have followed me, but we both know it doesn't matter, and anyway, this isn't the point he's trying to make.

"It wasn't his security detail," he tells me with a sigh. "And it wasn't one of us."

"So who was it?" I ask, because even if the shoe doesn't fit, Henry wants you to shrink into it.

His eyes close slowly before opening again. When they do, they pin me in place. It's as though he is looking straight through me. Finally, he shakes his head. "That," he says with a mirthless flash of teeth, "is the million-dollar question."

I start to speak, to say something, to say anything—to prove that this isn't as big of a deal as he's making it. But before I can form the words, he steps forward and grabs my wrist, and something in his eyes stops me. That something, whatever it is, reminds me of the Italian with the watch. It takes me back to that first kill, reminding me how easily accidents can happen. It's all reflected there now, a warning or a premonition, I'm not sure. "It's dangerous to go digging around in the past, Liv. You know that."

When I don't offer the rebuttal he is expecting, Henry raises my wrist, and motions for me to flatten my palm. He slaps his phone into it. "Geoffrey Dunsmore," he nods. "You might recall—the reason we flew to Fort Lauderdale."

My eyes shift from Henry's to the screen. Our passenger, who is inconveniently running late, stares back at me.

I take in the close-set eyes, the oversized nose, and backward smile. Then I glance up at Henry. "I am not as good at forgetting as you might think."

It's an olive branch, the photo. "Quite the colorful history, he has." Henry's expression and his tone tell me that he's willing to forget my little excursion, at least for now. They tell me he's calmed down, that he wants to focus on the job at hand. Henry is a professional, first and foremost. But it's more than this, I realize. He detests men like Geoffrey Dunsmore.

"The hit," I say. "Who contracted it?"

Henry avoids my question by leaning down and rubbing at a smudge on a window, which only makes it worse.

The truth is it doesn't matter. I'm aware of Dunsmore's history. I've read his file. Twice. Child pornography, statutory rape, and enough family money to make those things go away.

Still, this doesn't dull my curiosity.

When Henry—who has now devoted himself to properly cleaning all of the windows, going from row to row—finally looks up, disappointment is strewn across his face. "You know better than to ask that."

My brows rise. "Apparently not."

"Even if I knew—you know I can't say."

"Just want to know how far I'm allowed to take things."

"What does it matter?"

"I'd bet it matters to his victims and their families a lot."

"Enough with the questions." He checks his watch and then looks back at me. "You're hurt. You need to be careful, Liv. Things could have gone really badly today. They still can."

"I was—I *am* fine."

"Last night must have been rough."

"No—why would you say that?"

"You're limping."

"I'm not."

Henry sighs heavily. "From now on, just stick to the plan, all right?"

The plan is simple: Henry's job is to slip a little Rohypnol into Dunsmore's scotch before takeoff. By the time we reach cruising altitude, I'll slip my gloved hands around his rather large neck and squeeze until his eyes pop, until the blood from biting his tongue creeps out of the side of his mouth, until the life drains from his bones. That's how Henry pictures it. And me too, to a certain extent. Of course, that isn't what actually happens.

CHAPTER TEN

Charlotte

One thing about psychopaths, they're incredibly perceptive. It's evident in Geoffrey Dunsmore's expression as he introduces us to his niece. "This is Clara," he offers with a vacant look.

He glances over at me. His expression turns curious, and he is very obviously awaiting a response. When it comes in the form of a tight smile, he shifts his attention to the girl. Another thing about psychopaths: they're like wild animals; it's important to hold your own. It's a matter of life and death. And even still, sometimes they win. A thought that is never too far from my mind.

Although we met once, years ago, Geoffrey Dunsmore doesn't appear to place me. But then, I haven't positioned myself in a way that he would. While Henry was busy sulking and scrubbing windows, I was working on a transformation of another kind. I shed the wig and the glasses and switched out the green contacts

I'd worn to lunch in favor of murky brown ones. For good measure, I added thick-rimmed glasses, swept my hair up into a French twist and changed into my uniform.

"Nice to meet you, Clara," Henry says, ushering the girl toward a seat. It gives me the time I need to really take her in. Her hair is disheveled. Not dirty, but not exactly clean either. Her clothes are ill-fitted. Her eyes disclose a fear that is contained.

She offers Henry a nod that is nearly imperceptible.

I place her at about fourteen—older than Hayley, younger than Sophie. It's hard to tell, especially these days, and to come right out and ask would be taking the kind of risk I can't afford.

Henry glances over his shoulder toward me. I see instantly what he wants to convey: a warning. Our plan hadn't accounted for the girl. It shouldn't be a surprise that Geoffrey Dunsmore has brought a guest along, but it is.

"Can I get you something to drink?" I ask, my voice a little off, a little too high-pitched, the mother in me coming through loud and clear. None of this goes unnoticed by Henry. His annoyance is written all over his face. "Are you hungry?"

The girl's eyes flit toward Geoffrey Dunsmore.

"She'll have water," he answers. "We've just come from a late lunch."

Taking his seat, he offers a bellied chuckle. "I'll take a scotch on the rocks."

As I prepare the drinks, Henry stands at my shoulder, alternating between glaring at me and peering into the cabin. "We can't take the risk, Charlotte."

I give him the side eye. Henry never calls me by my real name. Flight attendants should be like strippers he said once, early on. You play a part. The rest, no one needs to know. Later, after I'd officially accepted the role he offered, I understood what he meant. By that point, I realized it was a part of it. He had been warming me up all along. Turning me into what he wanted me to be. Henry has a way of doing that, which is unprecedented. But by then it was too late. I'd already become someone else. Codename: Olivia.

"She's just a girl," I say. "I'd hardly call her a risk."

It's a lie, and it comes out sounding like one. Henry folds his arms across his chest. "No witnesses—you know that."

"I'm not letting him off this plane with her."

He looks at me, appalled. "Then we'll have to kill them both."

I force an apologetic grin. "No."

"She's going to die either way."

"I'm not killing the girl," I say. "And you aren't either."

"How do you want to play it?"

"She's not his niece. You know that. And I know that."

"We all know that. So what? It changes nothing. She's a witness at best, a liability at worst."

"I don't—"

"You take him," he quips. "I'll handle her."

My palms start to sweat. I think it over and then shake my head.

The captain pops by, and Henry's nastiness vanishes. Once he leaves, Henry shifts gears and, trying to offer something kind, he leans in, his eyes radiating sympathy. "I'm sorry, Liv. We don't have a choice."

Placing the drinks on a tray, I maneuver around him before briefly turning back. Thinking of my father, I say, "We always have a choice."

CHAPTER ELEVEN

Charlotte

We land early enough that I am home in time for the take-out Michael has ordered for dinner. We made good time today, even considering how long it took to get Henry off the plane and safely into bed. Rohypnol is a powerful drug. Good thing I'd only slipped a fraction of the required dose into his coffee.

Something, no doubt, I'll have to answer for later. Something I'll deny, but still. I put it on my list of problems I need to figure a solution for. I trust Henry. But not enough to bet my life on it. There are limits, even for me, when it comes to breaking the rules.

In my defense, I wasn't thinking clearly at the time. Not only was I tired, but I didn't have all the facts. Henry will see this as weakness, as will the higher-ups, even though that's not what it was at all.

I didn't feel up for the extra work that a double kill takes. By the time I was aware we'd be transporting not one, but two passengers, I'd already dosed Henry up. The last thing I wanted was to have to argue about what happened at Estero the entire flight home.

Enclosed spaces and all, we were in a metal capsule hurling through the air. There's really nowhere to go.

Thankfully, Henry shouldn't remember too much of the details. His memory will be foggy, and I'll help fill in the dots. Also, I found out where Dunsmore is staying. Plan B—knowing I'll get to make a late night excursion helps lift my mood, if only slightly.

This way, I can get both Henry and the agency off my case. When all is said and done, I'll have taken care of Dunsmore and spared the girl's life.

I play the scene out in my mind, over Thai food, which I pick at but don't eat. Looking at my own daughters is distracting. I'm thinking about what that girl is going through when Hayley exclaims she is supposed to take brownies for Home Ec class tomorrow.

I may be preoccupied but not enough to miss how counterintuitive this seems. Michael comments, saying as much. When she claims it's for a taste test, to see who can tell which brownies are store bought and which are homemade, I know without a doubt that it's complete and utter bullshit.

"I'll take her to the store," Michael offers, sensing my agitation. "But you're helping with the baking—otherwise I can guarantee the results of that taste test."

"I was planning to go to the gym. It's a box recipe," I say. "How hard could it be?"

He glares at me over his Pad Thai. "Tough day?"

"Just long."

"Well, at least you have a few days off."

I rub at my eyes, silently detesting his unwarranted optimism. "Actually, I picked up a flight tomorrow."

When I look up, his face says everything I need to know, so his words don't have to.

"I'm sorry," I tell him staring into my soup. "They're desperate, Michael."

He drops his fork and pushes away from the table. "I know the feeling."

I don't move to follow him. Space and time are powerful forces and often necessary ones when it comes to getting what you want. I know how this works. I know how he works. Years of experience have to count for something.

I know exactly what will happen later. He'll offer his version of an apology. He'll say something simple. Something like, "I know you're devoted to your job. But we miss you when you're gone."

I'll sigh, sidle up close to him, and respond the way I'm supposed to, even if it's not the way I actually feel. I'll tell him I miss him too.

"Do you?" he'll ask as his hand trails down my back, eventually finding my ass. Maybe he'll want mercy sex, maybe it's a sign of submission. But more likely, it's only packaged that way. He's asserting himself, claiming both his position and me. I won't care. I'll kill it either way.

"You know I hate being away from you and the girls," I'll tell him, the lies dripping effortlessly from my lips.

His fingers will relax before stretching out again as he toys with the edge of my panties. For sure, I won't let the moment go to waste. "I'm sure business will pick up for you in the New Year and then I can cut back."

His hand will drop, and he'll tell me we don't need the money that bad. His lies won't come so easily.

I'll pull back and look him in the eye. "I know," I'll say. "It's just...who knows what the economy is going to do? Your work is slow as it is, and I don't think I could handle another 2008. Could you?"

He won't be able to argue against uncertainty, so most likely he'll say nothing. "You do so much for us," I'll tell him, knowing I have hit a nerve. My husband does not take rejection well. Never has. Mostly though, he doesn't like being reminded that we need my income.

I'll slide my hand up his shirt. A peace offering, both the gesture and the way my suggestion is posed. "Let me take Hayley."

He won't turn me down, which is good, because as it turns out, I have a little catching up to do with my daughter. She doesn't realize I survey data for a living, that I spend my days deciphering code, reading people, and so when it comes to where my children are concerned, it's like a walk in the park.

Until it isn't.

She's not a good enough liar. Yet.

CHAPTER TWELVE

Charlotte

The brownies aren't for home economics. They're for a little twerp named Elliot Brown who talks down to my daughter and frequently requests that she send pictures of her tits. I would kill the little fucker myself but, given what I have on my plate, it might be better to fire off a warning shot than to go full-bore right out of the gate. Some wins take time.

I haven't a clue what would make my daughter interested in a boy like Elliot Brown, but I know that if this kind of behavior isn't nipped in the bud straight away, I'm in for a lifetime of blood on my hands.

We're on aisle ten. I'm looking at laxatives while Hayley furiously taps away at her screen. We've already had a fight in the brownie aisle and currently aren't speaking, but that will just make the discussion on the car ride home that much more enjoyable.

I'm in the process of trying to decide Ex-Lax or Dulcolax

when a loud sound causes a jump scare that nearly buckles my knees.

It's unmistakable. The sound of gunfire. Rapid, unrelenting gunfire.

"Get down!" I command as shots ring out, rendering my voice useless.

Her eyes are wide, but her fingers punch furiously at her phone. She stands frozen. "Oh my God."

"What are you doing?" I hiss, grabbing her forearm and forcing her to the floor.

"Texting Dad."

I grip her elbow hard enough that she releases the phone. It drops to the tile. I pick it up and shove it in my purse. "Your father isn't going to save you," I say, crouching down beside her. "And neither is that fucking phone."

Pulling my Colt Combat from my bag, I tell her to stay low.

"Mom?" Her mouth drops and hangs open. "Why do you have a—"

"Don't worry," I assure her. "You're going to be fine."

Sweeping the safety down with my thumb, I take Hayley by the hand, and lead her toward the back of the store, away from the gunfire.

It's relentless, and it's growing louder and closer. My mind processes the scene quickly. Gunpowder. The screams. Bodies hitting the polished concrete. Pleas. Low moans. The metallic scent of fresh blood. Cries for help. Fear. I register it all.

We manage to make it down several aisles, venturing toward the stock room and the loading docks, before the gunman pauses to reload.

We are hovering behind the deli counter, a mere five steps from the stock room entrance, when I spot a woman and a young toddler hiding behind a cardboard display adjacent to where we are crouched.

Something about the boy reminds me of Sophie. It's the pajamas, I eventually realize. She was obsessed with a pair exactly like the ones he is wearing when she was that age. They have little trains on them, and if my memory serves me correctly, the little trains glow.

The thought stops me in my tracks. I glance from the boy to his mother, who is in shock, wild-eyed, and probably unmovable. "Over here," I say, motioning with my pistoled hand.

Panic registers in her eyes as they fix on mine. Almost imperceptibly, she shakes her head.

I tell her with my eyes and my mouth, with my entire body to send the boy in my direction.

Her eyes flit from one side of the store to the other. Shots ring out like fireworks on the Fourth of July.

"You have to move," I call out to her. "Or you are going to die."

Hayley clutches my sweater in her fist. The fire ceases momentarily. I feel her pulse reverberate in my ears. "Mom, come on."

The gunfire resumes. Closer this time, *too close*. I realize he wasn't just reloading, he was on the move. "Go," I instruct Hayley, eyeing the back door. "Now."

"I can't," she cries.

"It's sixteen steps," I tell her. "You can."

She clutches me tighter, pulling my shirt so that it's half hanging off of me.

"Go." I listen as between rounds the thick rubber soles of the gunman's boots squeak as they move along the tile floor. "I'll be right behind you."

In the oval mirror fixed in the corner of the ceiling, I spot the top of the gunman's capped head. With a shove and a reassuring nod, I shove Hayley toward the exit. Then I turn and motion to the woman one last time.

Sensing that it's her final chance, as people tend to do when faced with death, she peels away at the little boy's grip on her. I watch her lips move as she tells him to run to me. He does as she says.

But then he stops.

His eyes are like the rest of his little body. Frozen.

I wave with both hands, trying to get him to move.

Amid the chaos and the sound of rounds being shot off, I feel the boots closing in on us.

Darting from behind the meat market counter, it takes me three strides to reach the kid. Scooping him in my arms, I make a beeline back to the cover of the counter. We crouch, huddled together. The boy weeps silently.

Until he doesn't.

You can barely just make out his cries over the sound of bullets spraying. Over and over, he screams just one word: Mommy. Just beyond the chaos and the carnage, my brain registers what is about to happen.

Cupping my hand over his mouth, I glance toward the display where he and his mother had been hiding.

Looking back at me, I see eyes that mirror my own. The woman, sensing her child is about to be killed, lets out the most guttural cry I have ever heard, the kind that lodges itself into your brain and never leaves.

She has the gunman's attention. As he trains his gun on her, I fling the boy aside.

In my periphery, I watch as she makes the worst and most natural mistake possible. She attempts to flee in the direction of her child.

A flurry of gun shots ring out, some of which are my own.

I manage a hit to the groin, disappointing, but I do have a screaming toddler clinging to me, digging tiny fingernails into my bare leg.

Just as the gunman steadies his gun on me, and I know we are goners, someone attempts to tackle him from behind, knocking him off balance.

This gives me the fleeting second I need to get off a chest shot. I fire once, a direct hit, and watch as he goes all the way down, his rifle spraying bullets at the florescent lights overhead.

Within seconds, I find myself standing over him, his eyes fixed on mine. The light slowly draining out of them, it's apparent in the way that his fingers can no longer grip his gun. I nudge it away from his body with my foot, while simultaneously aiming my own at his head.

For a fraction of a second, I glance back at the woman sprawled out on the tile, her small basket beside her. Inside, a single package of diapers. The boy's head rests on her chest. Blood pools around them. "He had trains on his pajamas," I say and fire the shot.

CHAPTER THIRTEEN

JC

She attended to me with a flippancy I found unnerving, despite my desperation to be attended to. That's how I first came to know her, on a long haul flight.

She wasn't old, but she wasn't young, and I couldn't help but wonder what a woman like her was doing in a job like that.

I spent the majority of the flight watching her when she wasn't looking, which as it turned out was most of the time. I came to know the smooth curve of her neck, studying the spot where it connected at the spine. Her flat stomach was something that could be appreciated, and to top it off, I found it quite appealing the way her breasts rounded out that hideous uniform.

Her chestnut hair, possibly the only fake thing about her, was tied neatly up, resting gently at the base of her skull. Her eyebrows are perfection, neither too thick nor too thin, not like you see on most women. She wasn't beautiful in the striking kind of way, but more subtly, in the natural kind of way.

If I had to pinpoint one thing that both gave her away and solidified it for me...it would have to be the faint crease etched in the skin between her brow. She's a deep thinker, something I find suitable to my tastes.

She didn't seem to notice me watching. That or she didn't care. In her line of work, she's probably used to it. I couldn't yet tell, so I focused on the things I knew. First principles and all. Her nose, slightly up turned, was a little too small for her face but preferable over the alternative. However, it was those eyes that captured and held my attention more than anything. Heavy-lidded, somewhere between blue and green, like the ocean on a cloudy day. And don't get me started on that mouth of hers. It's indescribable. I'd better not try.

Straight-backed and purposeful, it was captivating the way she walked the aisle. Every now and again, she'd let out a small sigh, as though there was really something else she'd rather be doing.

Inevitably, I started trying to figure out what that something else was.

Like I said, it was a long flight.

Straight away I knew that she was married. She wore a simple gold band, tasteful and understated. It bothered me in the sense that a woman like that should have more, should want more, but it made her interesting in that she apparently didn't.

I hadn't thought that she might have children. A wife, I could picture her in that role. The kids were a curveball I hadn't seen coming. She didn't seem like the motherly type. It's funny the way you think you know a person and then out of nowhere they go and surprise you.

I suppose that's where it all started, with the curveball. A seed was planted and with it the decision was made. I had to follow her. It was supposed to be a one-off thing. Just to see what new bit of information I might get out of it. It wasn't like I was stalking her. I was curious, is all.

It was simple stuff I watched her do at first. Mundane things, everyday things. Things like dropping her daughter at school. I found it amusing, the way she practically shoved her out with a distant smile. At the gas pump, I studied her profile and noted the way she pulled a cloth from her backseat, careful not to touch the handle. I couldn't help but wonder if she was always so discreet.

I followed her to the airport. She brakes hard, follows too closely, and drives just above the speed limit. I worry about her on the road. I worry about her everywhere.

That's why, despite the shit show that it turned out to be, I was glad I was there in the grocery store that evening. Anti-stalking laws aside, if it weren't for me, she'd be dead.

CHAPTER FOURTEEN

Charlotte

Where you're supposed to be is on a plane bound for Chi-town, on a cloudy day, with terrible weather. You don't mind because you're doing what you were born to do and you're getting paid to do it.

Me, I'm standing at the bottom of the stairs in the foyer that's covered in flowers and cards in a home that doesn't feel like my own. But only in a physical sort of way. The rest of me is I don't know where.

On that plane headed for O'Hare, maybe. In that bloody grocery store, perhaps. In the school auditorium, occasionally.

It's a double-edged sword, fame is. One day you're shopping for the perfect laxative in which to dose your teenage daughter's crush, just to prove a point, and the next you're bombarded with reporters trampling your lawn. Suddenly, life is magnified. *Lights, camera, action.*

Suddenly, you're a character in your own life. And the rest of your family is the supporting cast.

The doorbell rings again. I don't move to open it. What's the point, if they just keep coming? Not that I can blame them. The well-wishers. It's a circus around here, and everyone loves a good sideshow. They all want to know how we're doing. *Considering.*

I can't come right out and say it, but personally, I feel fine. Well, fine if you ignore the fact that I've become a glorified prisoner in my own home. Media tents and trucks line the block. The neighbors have delivered endless casseroles and flowers and still they don't seem even half as put out as I am about all of the extra sets of eyes canvassing the neighborhood.

As Henry advised, I've refused all interviews. Or at least I had until yesterday, when I was so desperate to get out I agreed to visit the elementary school Sophie and Hayley attended. I should have said no. I know that. But I needed to get out. I needed to get to that hotel and wrap my hands around Geoffrey Dunsmore's throat.

Call it cabin fever, call it murderous rage, call it not wanting to leave a job undone. Call it what you want. Henry will surely be pissed. But students at that school are grieving the loss of two classmates, one of whom happened to be shopping with his dad, who was also a teacher there.

The older of his children died holding strawberries as his father tried to shield their bodies with his.

I don't know why this matters, but reporters keep asking me what I saw on the way out of the grocery store, once SWAT had arrived. They all want to know the same thing: if I got a gander at the kid clutching the strawberries.

I hadn't actually. But I did see a kid Sophie's age with a hole in his stomach the size of a man's fist, still pumping out blood. I did see an elderly man with half his face shot off, but somehow his death isn't what they want to hear about, even though the details are quite gruesome, because, you know, a life well-lived and all.

Anyway, at the school they let the students ask the questions. The event was broadcast live. On the replay, the ticker across the bottom hailed me as *Incredi-Mom* or *Wonder-Mom* or something like that, and I guess it's all about branding these days.

The point of visiting the school was to assuage the public's fear and to let the kids know that there are more good guys (even if they're women) than bad. The free clothes and the hair and makeup were nice incentives, I won't lie. I was asked not to bring up the fact that I used a gun to take the assailant down, nor has the media shown much interest in reporting that fact either.

It's better, I was coached, to let them think I stopped the assailant with my bare hands. Which I might have done, had I been able to get close enough. Which I wasn't able to do, not without my weapon, which I am thankful for, because without it there would be a lot more people dead, myself included. But no one wants to hear that. It detracts from the message, they said.

I'm a hero, they said.

I give people hope, they said.

The producers made a big point of mentioning several times that it's perfectly okay to cry on air. I'm not sure what that will solve and still I think back to yesterday, wondering if maybe I should have heeded their advice. If only I'd shed a tear…then maybe.

I imagine it playing out differently, like if I'd just said the right thing, if I'd just sniffled a few times this could all be over.

I replay the scene, picturing myself going through the motions. I see the kids seated on the floor of the cafeteria. I am on stage under hot lights, and all I can think about is being on that plane, arriving at O'Hare, killing the mark, waking up and doing it all again. It's the simple things in life that make you most happy. That is what I was thinking sitting there, my face broadcast around the world.

Fame is such a distraction.

I smile for the camera.

The irony does not escape me.

Neve Jordan, anchor of *Good Day America,* asks the audience if they have any questions for *Incredi-Mom.* One by one, I watch as tiny hands shoot up in the air. Most of the students want to know about superheroes, about what it's like, if I know any, until this one kid, the kid that ends it all, raises his hand. Suddenly, my face feels tight and frozen. My fake smile is plastered on, while my hands remain folded neatly in my lap. The kid stands up slowly, tilts his head, and says very curiously, "So what does it feel like to shoot a man in the face?"

I swallow hard, looking directly into the camera. I smile nervously as if to say, *kids these days.* And then I turn to him and answer honestly. "It feels really, really good."

CHAPTER FIFTEEN

Charlotte

The camera pans to the left and then to the right again, before shakily zooming in on the girl's face. Up close, she looks different. Younger.

Nonetheless, it's obvious who it is.

The girl on our flight from Fort Lauderdale to Austin.

Wearing nothing but a faded T-shirt and underwear that might have once been white, the transformation is shocking. For one, she's rail thin. Thinner than just a few days ago. Dirtier, too. Her knees are blackened. Dark circles outline her eyes.

Whatever they've done to her, it's drastic.

The camera shakes as a deep male voice orders her to remove the shirt. When it steadies and zooms in on her face, I notice a subtle shift in her eyes, a flicker of fear or surprise, maybe both, which causes my palms to instantly sweat. Wiping my hands on my silk trousers, I mentally catalog everything I can about the girl and the room and the voice.

It doesn't sound like Geoffrey Dunsmore, but I can't be sure.

"Nice pants," Henry says, drawing my eyes away from the screen. "What are they...Reiss?"

I smile. Henry looks out of place standing at my bar, his coffee mug untouched making it all too obvious idle chit-chat is not why he's come. "Yes."

"Well, they suit you. But it's strange," he says, rubbing at his chin. "I don't see how he doesn't see it."

I don't ask who he is talking about. I don't have to. Michael has driven the girls up to his mother's for the afternoon to get away from everything—namely, all of the foot traffic on our lawn. I stayed behind, feigning the need for a bit of quiet and, with any luck, a nap. "See what?"

"Nothing...never mind."

Shrugging nonchalantly, I pull out a barstool and motion toward it. "Sit."

I can tell he's still angry with me over the unfortunate events that took place during our last flight. But, I can also tell that this isn't the half of it. "It doesn't make any sense," Henry says, perching himself on the seat. "You're wearing three-hundred-dollar pants. Meanwhile, he's driving around in a beat-up Honda."

Refusing the bait, I tap the back button, rewinding the video fifteen seconds. The muffled voice plays again, seeping equally with desire and control. "You think he's using a voice changer?"

"It's possible."

As the girl pulls the T-shirt over her head, I watch intently hoping to see something I missed before, although *what* exactly, I'm not sure. A clue, a birthmark, anything.

"She can't be more than thirteen," Henry says, staring over my shoulder. The girl covers her chest with the crumpled T-shirt and both hands.

"Why are you here?" I ask, addressing the elephant in the room.

"You mean other than the fact that you've majorly fucked up?"

"Yes—other than that."

"Because I wanted you to see this."

I refuse to indulge Henry in his games. At least not in the way he wants. Which is why I don't respond. It's easier to let him drive his point home. Mostly because I'm aware this is not the only reason he's here, sitting in my kitchen, at my bar. This is Henry's way of once again making one of his points.

"Two guesses who's behind this?"

I give him a sideways glance. The truth is it could be anyone in the video. Sure, the M.O. closely resembles that of Geoffrey Dunsmore. Buy a girl, keep a girl, film the girl, discard the girl by whatever means strike his fancy. But that isn't saying much. This world is full of small time traffickers, but we're rarely paid to dispose of people involved with one of those. It's the more nefarious rings we're paid to infiltrate, those who have select clientele, those who are competition for one reason or another, those who think they're immune to getting caught—those who make a big production of it, like the one we are watching on Henry's phone.

The doorbell rings. Henry's eyes dart toward the front of the house.

"It's probably just a neighbor. You wouldn't believe how many friends I'm making."

Henry rolls his eyes. "Because that's exactly what you need."

"You have no idea."

The bell chimes again. I pull up the doorbell camera app on my phone. "Nope, it's someone from the media."

"How long can this go on?"

"I don't know."

"I saw the interview, by the way."

Shoving my phone in my pocket, I walk around the counter toward the coffee pot where I refill my mug. Eventually, I turn and meet Henry's eye. "Oh yeah?"

"Yeah—and well, let's just say you put yourself—you put all of us in a compromising position."

The coffee burns my mouth. I hardly notice. "What was I supposed to do?" I ask, considering how much time a hot cup of coffee might buy me. "I have a life, Henry."

"So?"

"So this is not what I expected either," I tell him, thinking about how it could just as easily be my daughter in that video, thinking about how sometimes you get too close to a thing before you realize the trouble you're in.

You have to be careful. Evil is like a dandelion that spreads and spreads until they're at your very own back door. Until they're in your kitchen. And worse, you realize you invited them there. "You think I asked for that guy to shoot up the supermarket? As you can see, there are people all over my lawn. Neighbors are coming 'round at all hours. I can't even leave the house."

"And yet somehow you thought talking to the media would help."

I take another sip of my coffee and consider the least messy way to murder Henry in my kitchen. I really like these pants. "I don't know. Maybe I did."

"Face it, Charlotte. You like the attention."

Considering the odds of killing a person in self-defense twice in one week and getting away with it seem slim, I offer a forced sigh. "I don't know what you want me to say. I never asked for any of this."

He motions around the room. "Didn't you though?"

I set the mug down, realizing the odds are probably not in my favor. Henry will have to die quietly. "What's your point?"

"My point? My point is you have no idea what it took to get in here."

He's wrong. I do know. I watched him scale the wall that surrounds our backyard. Henry in his fancy suit, not a hair out of place. Sometimes I am surprised by how much tougher he is than he looks. "I'm here because they want me to bring you in." He stabs at his phone. "Now."

"That's ridiculous."

"Maybe," he shrugs. "Although, who's to say? I'm just the messenger."

I was prepared for this. Still, despite everything, Henry siding with the agency stings. "Would they be happier if I'd gotten shot?"

"Did you really need to go on television?"

"I needed a way to get to Dunsmore. I needed to get out of this house. And I figured if I gave a statement—things would die down."

"You made a statement all right."

"It was live. I didn't plan it that way. I was...what do they call it? On the spot."

"Well, that was a fucking disaster if I ever saw one..."

I look away. "Tell them they're going to have to come to me."

"You know that's impossible."

"If I leave here with this circus on my lawn, there's a good chance I'll be followed. Tell them that."

Henry stares at me for a long time.

"You drugged me."

I sip my coffee, peering at him over the mug. "Me? Drug *you?*" I asked, knitting my brow. "Why would I do that?"

"You shouldn't lie to me, Charlotte." He nods toward a vacation photo of Michael and the girls that's stuck to the refrigerator. "I'm probably the only person who can see right through you."

"I cannot change your mind if it's already made up then, can I?"

Henry sighs heavily. I've called his bluff and he knows it. He can't prove anything, and at this point, it doesn't matter. He has a choice to make. He knows I won't go with him willingly. Nor will I stand by and let him tear my family apart. "I can't keep saving your ass, you know."

"I'm not asking you to. I'm asking you to tell a good story."

"Telling stories is not what they pay me for," he says before turning his attention back to the video.

I wait for him to say more, to argue, to make his move, but when he doesn't, I walk around the bar and lean in close. "You wouldn't hurt me would you, Henry?" I say, pressing my cheek to his shoulder, in precisely the kind of singsong voice I know he hates.

"Just watch the goddammned video, Charlotte. Otherwise I might."

It surprises me that he calls me by my real name a third time. Sometimes I doubt he even remembers. I take it as the positive sign that it is. I've gotten him emotional. I've made it personal. That's why he came. And that's how you win.

I place my hand on his forearm and give it a squeeze. "Do you not like my coffee?"

"I'm not a fan of drugs before noon," he retorts, and I laugh. Henry and I, despite our disagreements, we understand one another. He points at the screen. "Are you watching?"

"Of course." The girl glances from one side of the room to the other, and I realize there's someone else aside from her and the cameraman.

"Drop the shirt and turn slowly," a gruff voice just out of shot says.

Henry thinks watching this is going to count for something. I know better. It changes nothing. It tells us nothing. The room is bare. The walls are concrete, and the floor is carpeted. It's not cheap carpet, and still, it could be any room, anywhere. The camera zooms in on her face before pulling back. "Now," the man demands.

Henry and I watch as the T-shirt falls to the floor.

"She could be older," I say, even though I doubt it. "Fifteen...sixteen."

"A little slower," the man tells her. His accent is decidedly American. To me, it doesn't sound like Geoffrey Dunsmore.

The girl turns clockwise. When she faces the camera again, she is asked to state her name.

"Elena." It comes out as a whisper. The way her index finger scrapes back and forth against the cuticle of her thumb leads me to believe she's probably telling the truth. "And how old are you, Elena?"

Her gaze remains fixed on the floor. "Twelve."

"What do you want to be when you grow up, Elena?"

"A dancer."

There's a distinct rattling sound off camera before the video ends abruptly.

"Motherfucker," Henry spits. "This has Dunsmore written all over it. And yet—it gives us nothing."

"Not nothing."

"She'll be dead in forty-eight hours."

"She's dead now," I say.

Henry's eyes meet mine as he realizes I've gotten the point he has come here to make. This is not the first video of its kind we've seen. Nor will it be the last. It's certainly not the worst of them. "Maybe we should watch it again."

"We can watch it a billion times," I tell him, taking the phone. "And still it will be the same."

"What's that supposed to mean?"

"It means we have what we need."

"And what's that?"

"A reason to tell the agency to go to hell—to let me do my job. And for you to get the fuck out of my kitchen."

CHAPTER SIXTEEN

JC

She's not one of those people who shies away from the limelight, something I find equally surprising and fun to watch. It's charming, even slightly endearing, in a sad kind of way.

She pretends not to like the attention, although it's clear that she does, something that becomes very apparent when she gives the second interview. I don't think she means to offer herself up to the cameras in the way that she does, but there they are, happily camped on her lawn, after all. When she opens her mouth and tells the world what a terrible burden this all has become for her, it's almost like she becomes someone entirely new. *Fake. Fake. Fake.*

She certainly doesn't appear burdened, and it only looks like she's crying when she dabs at her eyes with the sleeve of her blouse and begs for space for her children's sake.

One thing is for sure: she's developed a pretty big jones for drama.

She wants privacy. But she looks phenomenal. Sensational. Like the kind of woman who could bring a madman to his knees. How misguided she is. I don't know who could turn away from that.

Not me, that's for sure. It's a beast that feeds itself, consuming her. No matter how much I watch, or how close I get, the feeling that I missed something remains. It's there, deep in the pit of my stomach, an itch or a longing, it's hard to tell, but there's the lingering notion that I haven't experienced all of her. Seeing that we can't be together all the time—not yet, anyway— I get a nagging feeling that I've rushed through moments when I should have been paying attention.

For a bit of perspective, I managed to dig up an old yearbook, back from her sophomore year of high school.

She was only featured three times. Once alphabetically—in the typical headshot type of photo, once for debate team (I should have guessed), and then there was the candid shot. That was the one that interested me most.

She was seated on a classroom floor, legs crossed, a slip of paper in her hand. Her hair was longer and lighter, her cheeks fuller, but otherwise she looks like a slightly younger version of the woman I'm coming to know.

I guess that's why I cut the photo out. I carry it with me.

It wasn't until today, until her second interview, that I saw the full potential of the situation. That's when I knew. I'm not going to rush this. I'm fully aware that it might take a long time to sort out what she means to me. Looking at her sitting crisscross apple-sauce in that candid photo, I realize it might be more than I had originally thought. Maybe even more than the others. Whatever the case, I want to be that photographer. I want to know her that intimately.

It's become important, both her and the photo, the kind of thing you wouldn't want to lose. Taking it from the pocket of my suit, I position it next to my computer monitor, and I stare at her face for a long time. It's funny how the things you most want turn out to be the things money can't buy. Tracing the outline of her face, I imagine us having breakfast, for the simple fact that it seems more intimate than dinner. She won't have to worry about intrusions. I'll make sure it's just the two of us in the restaurant. If privacy is truly important to her, that's what I'll give her.

I'll give her anything she wants.

Of course, I imagine us doing ordinary things, as well. Given enough time, I'm sure she'll share my hobbies. I picture us white-water rafting, bungee jumping, climbing Kilimanjaro. Knowing her, she'll probably insist on throwing something impetuous into the mix, something like deep sea diving. I'm claustrophobic, but I'll go anyway, because I'll be the only one watching.

Opening a new tab, I click over to the local news site. I hate that the media is bothering her so much, yet at the same time, I love how easy they are making things on my end. Every day a new detail is revealed. At the top of the latest story, is a video, the thumbnail features her standing in her driveway. Her house is one of the most unique houses I've ever seen, sleek and modern, nothing like I would have pictured.

I hated it from the first time I saw it.

I couldn't help but wonder if she likes it.

With a quick search, I got my answer. Her husband is an archi-tect; he designed the place. All of a sudden, it made sense. She couldn't tell him that she hates it, even if it's the truth. I picture it going up in flames, the fire eating away the memories, erasing the history, and maybe even him.

She won't be sad. Not for long. I'll build her a house that she adores, maybe with my own two hands. I've done a lot of things in my life, but not that. We'll design it together from start to finish and all will be right in the world, and she'll forget she ever lived in that other house, with that other guy.

CHAPTER SEVENTEEN

Charlotte

In every life, there's a moment, or rather, likely a series of them —say, the birth of a child, or an engagement, or a divorce—the kind of event where you realize that from that moment on, nothing is ever going to be the same again. This is, for me, one of those moments. Standing in the kitchen, my husband at my heels, listening to the slow drip of the coffee pot, my mind wanders. You can have pretty much anything instantaneously these days. Everything except coffee, apparently. Good coffee, Michael swears, takes time.

"Good morning," he whispers, wrapping his arms around my waist. His body firmly pressed against mine, he moves into position, pinning me against the counter. The stubble on his face grazes the back of my neck as he buries his face into my shoulder, his lips lingering on what we both know is my weak spot. "Morning."

"You're up early."

"Yeah." I'm contemplating what I've done, and then, pushing away from the counter, I turn to face him. "Couldn't sleep."

Our eyes meet briefly before he pulls me against his chest. My head rests perfectly in the space beneath his chin. "It's Wednesday," he says. "Did you forget?"

"No—"

"Good thing we don't have anywhere we have to be."

"Good thing," I tell him with a half-hearted smile. He has taken the week off to be with me and the girls. Ever since the shooting, he's been unbearably attentive, as though it has suddenly dawned on him that life is short and unexpected and then you die. This is essentially my worst nightmare. Every relationship has its own flavor. But, we are not, and never have been, that kind of couple. I am not looking to change that now, not this far in.

"Just think," he says. "We can do anything we want."

We cannot do anything we want. I press my lips together tightly. "Mmhmm."

He slips his hand up my shirt. "Have any ideas?"

I try to come up with something, with anything. "Um…"

No one tells you how hard it can be to occupy all the hours in a day. I know he's referring to sex, but without coffee coursing through my veins, I'm not feeling particularly creative. "I think I have an appointment."

"An appointment? What appointment?" He seems surprised, and then I realize why. "I took a peek at your calendar. I saw book club on there…but not anything about an appointment."

"Really?" It's actually surprising how clingy he's become, so unlike the man I've been married to for the last decade and a half. For days now, all he's done is wander the house, hovering, unsure what to do with himself or what to say. His insistence that we keep the girls home from school—to recover—has been less than ideal. They are bored, I am bored, and now Michael is bored. Nevertheless, he was adamant about it—even after I pointed out that almost all psychologists say sticking to a normal routine is best after trauma. I was overruled. Three to one.

It hasn't exactly helped that none of us can leave the house without being accosted. But this—all of this togetherness, being holed up in our home—doesn't exactly amount to privacy either.

"Maybe I'm wrong," I tell him, untangling our bodies, moving toward the window. The street is quiet but far from empty. "Maybe it's tomorrow."

"Didn't see anything about an appointment tomorrow either..."

"Maybe it's on my work calendar."

"Maybe," he says. "Or maybe you're just tired. You haven't slept in days."

"I slept a little. On the couch. Didn't wanna wake you."

"It's understandable, Charlotte," he replies with an edge I know. "You don't have to pretend everything is fine—when it clearly isn't."

"I know it isn't," I say with a nod toward the stairs. "Hayley isn't sleeping either."

After several long beats, he sighs. "I think we're going to have to talk about it, don't you?"

"We are talking about it."

"I mean—really talk."

Turning away from him, my eyes close slowly. I squeeze them shut and count to five, making sure to keep my voice calm and even. When it comes to lying, practice doesn't make perfect. There are always telltale signs. Tone is one of them. "What do you want to know?"

"Well, for one, I'd like to know how it is possible that my wife is basically a sharpshooter and I had no idea."

I knew that Michael was going to have questions about the gun, so this does not exactly come as a surprise. I turn to face him. "I'm hardly a sharpshooter. I shot him point blank."

"Jesus."

Chewing at my bottom lip, I realize his expression is why it's important to manage this conversation appropriately. I assumed he would want to know how I knew to shoot, where I got the gun, and why I had it to begin with. For the most part, the answers to those questions are easy. "It's really not a big deal. I'm fine—Hayley is fine—this will all blow—"

"You killed a man, Charlotte. You just said it yourself. You shot him point blank in the face. Who could be fine after that?"

"In the head," I say, correcting him.

He glares at me wide-eyed with his mouth slightly open.

"It wasn't exactly for sport."

"I know," he says crossing the kitchen. He takes my hands into his. "I'm sorry. I don't mean to sound insensitive. This is just a lot to take in."

You have no idea. "For me, too."

Michael's response gives me hope that this will in fact all blow over. Most people, Henry included, have a hard time believing that it's possible to hide what I do from my spouse. Especially, if you consider I've been doing it for so many years. But that's because people these days have forgotten what discretion truly is. Privacy is power. What people don't know, they can't ruin.

It's always funny to me. People *think* they know what their spouse does when they're outside the house. But do they really? Eight, ten, twelve hours a day—sometimes more—the person you share a life with leaves home and essentially lives another life, fulfilling a role, earning a living, being someone else, doing something else. Believe me, I've stewarded enough flights to know. We all wear different masks.

"Maybe," he suggests, "We could run through it. Perhaps it would help if you talked to someone—if you talked to me."

"I don't know if I'm ready for that, Michael." I take a deep breath in and hold it. Obviously, I'm aware that I can't fend off his curiosity forever. But so far, I've managed okay, and I'd like to keep managing. "You have no idea what it was like. The gunfire... all those people... all that blood."

"You can talk to me, you know."

You hate blood. "I know."

"I need you to talk to me."

"I am." *You don't really want to know.* "We're talking."

"Why did you have the gun, Charlotte?"

I don't want to answer, but I can't just let us stand there locked together in silence. I know he'll wait for the answer longer than I can wait to give it to him. Still, I don't trust my voice. I have the distinct feeling that if I lie to him, he'll somehow know.

With a deep sigh, I scoot around him and open the refrigerator door in search of something to fix for breakfast. "One of the girls at work was attacked a few months back." Taking a carton of eggs from the shelf, I turn so we are facing one another. "And I don't know—I just thought I should protect myself."

"Attacked?" His eyes widen. "What? Why didn't you say anything?"

I shrug. "It wasn't really a big deal, I didn't think. I mean...it didn't happen *at* work. But *after*—well after—she talked about how she'd bought a gun and was thinking of taking a class—and so a few of us went together. To show our support. "

"You took a class? When?"

"I don't know. A few months ago...back in September...I think."

"And you didn't think that you might want to mention this at some point?"

"It wasn't like I was hiding it." I place the eggs on the counter. "It just never came up."

"Hold on." He's pacing now, and going over to the doorway, he stops and glances around the corner. Then he looks back at me, his voice lowered. "Let me make sure I have this right. You brought a loaded weapon into our home—you carried it day in and day out, in your purse—and it just never came up?"

"Not *every* day."

His eyes blink rapidly as he tries to piece it all together.

"Look," I offer, changing tactics. "I know how you feel about my job, and I didn't want to worry you. I didn't want to make things worse."

In two strides, he's at the window. Bracing himself against the counter, he stares out at the media trucks lining our street. "You didn't want to make things worse..."

"My dad was a cop—having a gun around was just a normal thing for me growing up. It wasn't something we felt we needed to discuss, Michael. It just was."

"Well, I'm not your father."

"Then stop acting like it."

When he turns, his expression is pained. "What's that supposed to mean?"

"If I hadn't had the gun," I say, retrieving the bacon from the fridge, "we wouldn't be having this conversation." I slam the bacon on the counter. "Your daughter and I—we'd be dead."

"Fine. Where are we supposed to do the grocery shopping? It shouldn't take that long to get things cleaned up, right?"

I glance at him sideways. This is not the question I'd expected. "I have no idea."

"I'd hate to have to drive across town," he answers with a nod toward the window. "I'm not even sure I can get out of the drive."

The best I can manage is a tired nod. I'd give anything to drive across town without being followed or noticed or both.

"We're low on coffee creamer."

"I'll text Julia. See if she'd mind picking some up."

Julia is our neighbor, two houses down. She, too, has been helpful since the shooting. But then, she's divorced, unemployed, and very obviously a big fan of my husband, so I suppose you could say she's always rather helpful.

Michael backs away from the window, picks up a stack of mail on the counter and skims through it. Then he looks up at me. "It's basically fan mail."

Cracking an egg into the frying pan, I hit it a little too hard and have to go fishing for tiny bits of shell.

"How long do you think fifteen minutes of fame lasts?"

"I don't know," I say. It's something I've been wondering myself. Yesterday, when I took Sophie to her basketball game, I was asked for my autograph. Twenty-six John Hancocks later—I know because Hayley counted—I had to excuse myself. And that was before the game. After, there was a mob of people waiting. We had to exit through the locker room, and even then, it was nearly impossible to get to the car amid the swarm of onlookers.

Then, last night, Henry sent me an email with a link to a social media account created in my honor. Several clicks later, I stumbled upon a closed group devoted to other women who want to take matters into their own hands. Vigilante justice at its finest. An eye for an eye, or something like that, as the saying goes. According to Henry, meetings are springing up all over the place, in thirteen countries so far. Self-defense classes, target practice, basic surveillance...you name it, these meetings are all-inclusive.

I wasn't sure what Henry wanted me to do with the information. Actually, I hadn't planned to do anything. But then, the deeper I went, and the more misinformation I read, the more I couldn't help myself. I had to comment. What harm could it do to set up a fake profile and offer up a few pointers? I just wanted to set the record straight.

It started with basic stuff, like how to inflict fatal wounds, knives that are easy to conceal, how to properly dispose of a body, the best silencer on the market, what to do if your gun gets jammed, those sorts of things.

By the time dawn rolled around, my post had been shared so many times my account had tens of thousands of followers. It hadn't even really hit in the U.S. by that point. Most Americans were still asleep.

I'm eager to check it now. Michael sniffs the air and then walks over to the burner and turns down the heat. I watch the bacon sizzle in the frying pan, burning, because my mind has been elsewhere. There's no telling how far I could take this.

What else am I supposed to do with all of these endless hours? If I can't leave the house, if I can't do my job, if I can't yet get to Dunsmore myself, the least I can do is minimize the damage by empowering the masses.

CHAPTER EIGHTEEN

Charlotte

The pure sound of the ball pounds the wooden court. The swish of the net remains unmistakable. "Way to go Sophie!" Michael shouts. We're seated side by side in the gymnasium, so I have to be careful. Something that becomes apparent when he looks over at me and frowns at the phone in my hands. "She just scored. Were you even watching?"

"Of course, I'm watching." I glance down at the court and find Sophie, her faced fixed in concentration as a teammate slaps her back.

"Good," he murmurs, turning his attention to the scoreboard. "Just making sure."

My phone vibrates in my hand signifying a new comment has been added. I uploaded some new tradecraft tips into the Vigilante group and the questions are pouring in. The squeak of tennis shoes chirp and give flavor to the answer I type. Basketball is a glorious game. A sport that can be seen by the blind. It's pure energy, athleticism, with nothing to hide behind. There are no helmets to hide the faces. No pads to hide the body. There is no right fielder in basketball. Everything is laid out in front of the spectator. The game invites itself to your imagination. It seems nothing separates you from the players on the court. They move gracefully from spot to spot. It becomes clear why they're *there* and you're *here*. When Sophie leaps for the rim, it's as if she soars. Her awe-inspiring athleticism is enough to make my husband leap similarly from his seat.

Its simplicity is almost too much for me to handle.

"You aren't watching," Michael says, nudging me with his elbow.

"I am." Rhythmically, the ball moves up the court. Through the hoop it goes—this time it's the opposing team who scores—and back we go again. Sophie gets the ball. She shoots and misses. Michael cheers anyway. It goes on as though only a timer could hold us back from eternity.

"I know you hate this," he seethes, speaking under his breath. "But could you at least pretend."

"I don't hate it," I say, stuffing my phone in my jacket pocket. This is not a lie. I've always found the game interesting. There's no way to hide the player who can't shoot. Eventually, she will be left open, exposed, as if she's dared to put one toward the hoop. If she obliges, she seems to face her demons. The shot will fly, and she will likely be defeated. Statistics are statistics for a reason. If the ball clangs, it's par for the course. However, the opponent will have won.

"THAT'S MY GIRL!" I turn and look at my husband as Sophie scores once more. He's all lit up, and I think about how we all lie, maybe most of all to ourselves.

I HADN'T EXPECTED TO EVER SEE HIM AGAIN. BUT I SUPPOSE IT WAS meant to be this way. The best life has to offer often happens out of the blue. I didn't recognize him straight away. If I had, undoubtedly I would have passed the table along to one of the other servers.

"It's you—" he said, after I'd rattled off the daily specials. When he glanced up at my name tag, his face fell.

"I'm sorry," I said, but of course, I recognized him then. That smooth voice. Those dimples, the same hopeful eyes.

"You look like someone—" he stammered. "I thought you were someone else."

The way he looked at my giant belly, I could tell he was doing the calculations in his head. "Are you sure your name isn't Olivia?"

I tapped my name tag, pressed my lips into a tight smile and shook my head.

He seemed unfazed, meanwhile his colleagues looked slightly uncomfortable. Men seem to have a keen sense when another man is about to make a fool of himself. "I looked for you, you know. No one seemed to know who you were. It was like you disappeared into thin air—like you'd never existed at all."

"I'm sorry," I said with a polite frown. "I think you have me mistaken."

"I even went to the school directory." He shook his head as though he were trying to rid himself of an errant thought.

He was relentless, just like he'd been at the party. I didn't answer him.

Instead, I asked for their drink order and then, for the most part, ignored the table all together. When it came time to pay, Michael grabbed the check. He left a generous tip and along with it, his business card. On the back he wrote: *I don't care why you lied. Call me. Please.*

I tore up the card and tossed it in the trash. I didn't have time for a distraction. What I did have was a plan, and I was counting the days until I could see it through. All I could think about was getting back to the skies, getting back to real life. The pregnancy was just a blip, a short detour.

I'd picked out birth parents, a lovely couple who wanted what I wanted—a closed adoption.

What's that saying about the best laid plans? Well, it's true. About three weeks after that first lunch, Michael came back. He requested my section, and this time he was alone. "You never called."

I shrugged.

"I'd like to take you out."

"Excuse me?"

"You're not married, are you?" he asked, motioning toward my hand. "I mean, you're not wearing a ring." He glanced down at the menu. "Not that that matters. No one does things in order these days."

"Water? Coffee? Tea?"

"Whatever you're having."

"A baby," I said pointing at my enormous stomach. "I'm having a baby."

"Whew," he said. "I mean, I know the food is good here and all, but I'm really glad you mentioned it." He closed the menu and placed it on the table. "The elephant in the room, as they say." His eyebrows arched and he smiled. "You just never know."

I rolled my eyes and left the table. Eventually, after my boss insisted, I brought him a water. He looked like the simple kind, and I couldn't afford to be fired.

"So—Olivia," he said, glancing at the name tag. "Have I offended you?"

"No."

"Was our one-night stand *that* bad?"

"I can't recall."

"Ew," he said. "I'll take that as a yes."

"Can I take your order?"

"Another shot," he answered. "I'd like another shot."

"We don't serve alcohol before noon on Sunday."

"You know what I mean—I'd like a date."

"I don't think so."

"Why not?"

"I hate men."

"Oh, I believe that." He nodded at my belly and then he said, "Let's hope you're having a girl."

AFTER I DECLINED HIS OFFER, MICHAEL CAME BACK EVERY DAY thereafter, until I did eventually agree to have dinner with him. He invited me to his new house, the one we reside in now, the one he'd designed and built himself. It seemed he'd come a long way in just a few short months. But then, we both had. I'd nearly created a whole new life too.

He cooked for me, in his new kitchen, something Italian, and after that I guess you could say I never really left. He wasn't put off by the fact that I was hugely pregnant, which should have seemed strange, but you'd have to know Michael to really understand.

He told me that he'd never stopped thinking about me and that when you meet the right person you just know. A decade older, he assured me he was certain of what he wanted: a house and a family. I suppose to his mind, he was already well on his way to having half of that equation, and I was simply the missing piece. It was easy. People assumed the baby I was carrying was his. He never bothered to set them straight.

"She could be mine," he said to me one afternoon after we'd made love, his fingers drumming a soft beat on my belly.

"But she's not."

"I know. Believe me, I've worked the math every which way." He looked up at me and smiled. "But she could be."

I didn't say anything. Not for a long time. I thought of Dan, the pilot, her actual father. I thought of the emails that went unanswered, I thought of the last time I saw him, at the company Christmas party, and how he wouldn't look me in the eye. I thought of his wife's hand on my belly, and the smile on her face when she asked me when I was due.

I thought about the adoptive parents I'd selected, somewhere across the country, preparing for a child they might not ultimately have. "She could be," I said to Michael.

"Marry me," he said.

"Marry you?" I don't know if I was actually surprised or not, but I'd witnessed enough proposals to know that you're at least supposed to pretend.

"Yes," he grinned. "Marry me. It'll make the paperwork easier." He traced circles on my stomach. "That way, I won't have to adopt her. We can make it right from the beginning."

I didn't have the heart to tell him it was too late for that—that the beginning was about seven months ago—that I was constantly staring at it in the review mirror. So, I said the next almost-right thing: I said okay.

CHAPTER NINETEEN

JC

Let's see what she keeps in her panty drawer. I mean, since I'm here. I go carefully, the rest of the upstairs is dark. Best to keep it that way.

What do we have here? A little bit of everything. G-strings, bikinis, lots of lace. Nothing crotchless. Too bad.

Next, I move on to the bathroom and most importantly, the medicine cabinet. There's a couple of different kinds of creams, Vaseline, Tylenol. A box of Rogaine. *Interesting.* A half-full prescription bottle of Ciprofloxacin. *Shame.* An Epi-Pen, and next to it, a small bottle labeled escitalopram. Also known as Lexapro. *Oh, Charlotte.* Darling. *What could you possibly have to be anxious about?*

One thing that's missing is birth control. *But maybe you carry that with you? I swear, Charlotte. Every time I think I have you figured out, you reveal that I'm no closer to solving this mystery.*

On your side of the bed rests a stack of books. I know you

read. They aren't for show, not like the last woman I dated. I'm relieved to see that you're not like her, that there are bookmarks stuck between the pages, dog-eared corners, notes in the spine. I wish there were more time to read them all. Unfortunately, I don't have long. I'm not exactly sure how long high school basketball games last, but better to be safe than sorry. *Now excuse me while I check out your closet.*

It's shocking in here, and it's not. *Pretty expensive taste you have for a flight attendant.* There has to be at least fifty pair of shoes. Not the cheap kind, either. Manolos, Louboutins, Alexander McQueen, Gucci boots. *Where do you wear them? When do you wear them?*

Once I've properly checked out the Joneses' his and her closets, I move on to the real reason I came. Setting my backpack down, I carefully unpack its contents. That's when I feel it, snaking around my ankles, moving across the rug, back and forth.

Jesus, Charlotte. Why didn't you mention you had a cat?

"Here kitty, kitty," I murmur when my breathing returns to normal and the hairs on the back of my neck are once again at ease. I scratch the spot between its ear and its neck. I hate cats.

As soon as we've both had our fill of one another, which luckily doesn't take long, I get down to business, unpacking the four motion-activated digital cameras I brought, each no larger than the average shotgun cartridge. Once I've placed them where I want them, I'll connect everything up, and with a few clicks on my laptop, I'll have the live audio/video feed streamed directly to my phone. *And then I can see you whenever I want, darling Charlotte. I can watch you sleep. I can watch you bathe. God, I hope you're into baths. If nothing else, I can watch you simply breathe.* What a wonderful world this is. *How lucky I am to be in it with you.*

Before I leave, I do a quick sweep of the desk and laptop in the office. It belongs to Michael, and I'm assuming—no—I'm *hoping* I'll find some dirt.

What I find amounts to nothing. No iffy-looking emails. No

hidden folders. No porn. His history hasn't even been cleared in months. *I feel sorry for you, Charlotte, being married to such a boring man.*

My wrist twitches, and I check my watch. 6:52 p.m. Double-checking my bag, I look to see that I haven't forgotten anything, that I haven't left evidence behind.

I reach the back door when the lights in the front room come on. "Mom? Dad?"

My fingers pause on the door handle. I could stay, slip into one of the closets, hide under one of the beds. Parents shouldn't leave their kids home alone. Terrible things have been known to happen. The footsteps move closer. "Hello?"

The voice is pure and sweet. And very young. I think I probably ought to stay. But then, I remember the cameras. The Joneses really should be grateful they have me to keep an eye on things. Slowly, I turn the knob and slip out into the cold dark night.

CHAPTER TWENTY

Charlotte

Michael grips my waist, digging his fingers in as he moves me back and forth, back and forth. I think of the swings on the old play set in the backyard. The way you can move and move without going anywhere.

We may be fucking, but we certainly aren't speaking. In the midst of our worst fight in years, we're communicating our displeasure with heavy hands and long sighs, sweaty sheets and short tempers.

The argument, at the basketball game, which was not about just one thing but about *every* thing, left a sour taste in my mouth. But not enough of one to turn down sex.

It's all I can think of. And it had better help. This is shaping up to be one of those long and drawn out disagreements, the kind that could take years to resolve, and very well might— the kind you can only truly understand if you've been married long enough to wonder just how in the hell you could possibly have ended up in a relationship with a person you don't even know.

Slamming my hips into his pelvis, I realize he's right. It's infuriating how someone can be so familiar and yet so foreign at the same time. That's what he said when he saw the suitcase come out. I leave for a trip tomorrow, despite the fact that I'd promised to take the week off.

I hadn't lied. I did plan to take some time off. But that was before Henry passed on a lead on Dunsmore, from a very credible source. Besides, it's not like my husband is completely innocent either when it comes to work.

Just this morning he informed me that he invited a client to our home this afternoon, which he never does. Given the circumstances, especially with the reporters still camped on the lawn, I don't blame him. It proves a point. It gives me leverage. Work will continue to encroach, business does not stop. No matter the tragedy, the world still spins, life goes on.

Michael halts my movement abruptly, which would be annoying under any circumstance, but *now* that I've fallen into a comfortable rhythm? *Really?* This is the time he chooses to speak to me? He repeats his question a second time. "Why did you marry me?"

"Because you asked," I tell him earnestly, grinding my hips. Perhaps I should elaborate more, tell him what he wants to hear, but I can't bring myself to do it. He has to focus. He has to let me focus. I need this.

Ever since the shooting, each day has been a carbon copy of the one before. Nothing ever happens. And when something does happen, like the argument we're in, it seems like the only thing that has ever happened.

This isn't what I signed up for. I need space. I need room to breathe. I need to come. "Fuck me," I say, thinking of the knife tucked in the mattress, about how far I might be willing to take this if he refuses. "We can chit-chat later."

He backs away and then plops down on his back. Using my hands to press against his chest, I climb on top. His eyes close, and when they open, he looks up at me like he's never seen me before. "I don't understand you."

I roll my hips, shifting into a more comfortable position. "There's not much to understand."

"You're not like other women. I've always known this," he says with a sigh. "But it's suddenly become more apparent—and I don't know..."

I don't say anything in response; I simply raise up and lower myself onto him, the two of us falling into an easy cadence. Eventually I let my head fall back, but I am not altogether unaffected by his words. *Were they meant to be a compliment?* "Most women," he continues, "they want to talk about things. They want to fix them."

He's right. I've never understood women who rattle on incessantly, insistent on discussing every single bit of the minutiae life has to offer. They've always seemed strange to me—women who lunch with girlfriends, volunteer at school, women who spend their time running back and forth to endless appointments. But now, I'm starting to get it. I'm starting to understand what it feels like to fill a whole day up with nothing. "Is this good?"

When he sighs heavily, I know I have him.

"Goddamn it," he says, gripping my hips, reminding me not to take score too soon. He holds me into position.

"What?"

"That's all you have to say—you married me because I asked?"

This is what true cruelty feels like. "What do you want me to say?"

"Oh—I don't know—how about that you were in love with me? How about that you're *still* in love with me—that you can't imagine your life without me?"

I smile down at him. Something's up. Michael has always been a bit needy. But not like this.

"You swept me off my feet," I say, taking his hands from my hips. "Now, if you'll let me finish what *you* started."

"Do you still want to be married?" he whispers softly, after I've come. It was an incredible orgasm, earth shattering, the kind that's meant to solve things, and sometimes does. "To me?" It's a strange question, but also a perfect one.

Searching his eyes, taking him in, I lay my head on his chest. As I count his heartbeats, it occurs to me what I have to do. I realize that the only way to get what I want, to get on that plane, to do my job, to kill Dunsmore, is to hurt Michael in the process. So I say the only thing I can say, the only thing that makes sense. I tell him, "I'm not sure."

CHAPTER TWENTY-ONE

JC

It is evident that I have interrupted something, and thanks to the video recording sent directly to my phone, I know exactly what. I couldn't have planned the timing of our meeting any better, not even if I tried.

She looks radiant standing in the center of her kitchen. Barefoot, wearing jeans and a sweater, her hair is longer than I recall. Slightly wavy, it hangs loosely around her shoulders, accentuating the fact that her makeup is done tastefully. She belongs on the cover of a magazine.

"This is JC Clements," Michael says. "The client I told you about."

With a curt nod, I extend my hand. It's quite the quaint affair, being here in their home, all of us together. I imagined this to be exciting, thrilling even, but it feels nothing like that at all. Lips move, but I hear nothing, only a loud thrumming in my ears. My vision narrows, and all of a sudden, the air in the room seems insufficient to keep me alive.

"Charlotte," she says, taking my hand. "A pleasure." The warmth of her skin and the sound of her name forces air into my lungs. The room stops spinning. Her voice anchors me. Everything I've ever wanted comes into vivid focus. She is beautiful. I want to fuck her. I want to marry her. I want her to have my children. I decide it then. I love her with the kind of mad passion that I reserve for only one other thing in my life.

"Mr. Clements wanted to see the house, in person," he says to her.

Her eyes crinkle at the corners, and she sort of tilts her head and smiles. She's curious about me, but she doesn't force the questions that need to be asked. She doesn't say that she knows me, does not suggest that we have flown together several times. If she recognizes me, she does not let on. If she is surprised to see me in her kitchen, she is very good at not showing it.

"How wonderful," she tells him with a tight smile, before turning her attention back to her phone. We could be great together, I think, staring at her nails. Unpolished, they're trimmed neatly, rounded and filed, perfect in an unassuming kind of way. She looks up suddenly and catches me staring. "Wait..." she says, clicking her phone off. "I think we've met before."

I look over at Michael Jones. His brow is raised.

"I think you're right." If there's one thing a woman likes to hear, it's that.

Her head tilts as her eyes narrow. The way she sizes me up feels like floating in the ocean on a warm day. "Where?"

"Um...in the air, I think...I'm a flight attendant."

"Ah—yes," I say, pretending to place her. "You were on the flight to New York...?"

"Geneva."

"Oh—right. Forgive me. I fly a lot."

Another tight smile. "Me too."

She turns to her husband. "I'm giving an interview," she says. "Here, in the kitchen. We're on in five minutes."

"An interview?" he echoes, brow furrowing.

"Yes." She chews at her bottom lip. "I'm so sorry." Then she glances my way as though she's just remembered me standing there. "I forgot to mention it."

"I see." Michael Jones scans the kitchen. He stops when his eyes land on me, making it clear that he does not, in fact, see. "I'm afraid we might have to make this quick."

Her eyes shift between the two of us. They contain entire universes. Unnamed galaxies I'd like to explore. "I'm terribly sorry."

"JC is building. He thinks he might like something similar up on the lake. I thought I'd give him the grand tour."

She sort of nods like she isn't listening or she doesn't care.

"It's just a vacation home," I say, and how does love even work? "Not my main one." I should shut up, but she makes me want to talk.

I'm thinking— no—I'm *hoping* that she's going to ask me what I do, but she doesn't. She doesn't get the chance. One of their daughters, the oldest, wanders in. She says something to her mother, which I don't hear because I'm struck by how much the two look alike, now that I am seeing them up close, side by side.

"Shall I show you around?" Michael Jones asks, catching my attention.

"I can always come back."

"Would you mind?" Charlotte asks, and I love that she's extended the invitation. At the same time, Michael says, "We'll be quick."

The Joneses' place doesn't look much different in the light than it did in the dark. Although, with him in it, it looks worse than it does on camera. But maybe everything looks better from a distance, artificial and foreign. I follow Michael as he prattles on about features I don't care about. The only feature of this home I came to see is in that kitchen. Narrowly, from the living room, I can see her getting mic'd up. "It's terrible what happened," I say.

"Yes," he tells me, a sad tinge to his voice. His eyes dart toward the kitchen. "My wife has been quite shaken up."

"I can imagine."

"Forgetful, too," he says, almost embarrassed.

I watch the camera crew and the reporter as they countdown to go live. They ask questions about social media and copycat accounts and whether *this* Charlotte Jones is the same Charlotte Jones who has been rallying, asking for others to step up and take matters into their own hands.

She reminds me of a brunette version of Princess Diana sitting there opposite the hungry reporter. Charlotte has a pureness about her, a fair amount of charisma resides in those large doe eyes of hers. So demure, she is. Almost shy. Excellent at manipulation. Part victim, part instigator. But then, that's what makes the story so compelling. Dark and untimely, a tragic fairytale. "No," Charlotte says for the camera. "I would never."

"What do you think about all of this? The latest developments? The instant fame?" the woman asks. "You must have heard about the fan clubs cropping up."

"I try not to pay attention to any of it. To be honest, I've been very busy with my children. We're all still a little in shock."

The reporter's voice lowers. "This must be a very difficult time for your family."

"It has been—it is."

"Do you have anything you want to say—to these men and women who are committing criminal acts—to those that are setting halfway houses on fire—that are kicking in doors of parolees?"

"Not really."

You can see by the woman's face this is not what she expected, and definitely not the answer she was hoping for. Ambiguity hardly makes good television. "Not really?"

"Well—," Charlotte says. She sucks her bottom lip between her teeth like it's a maneuver she's practiced. "It's just that you have to be careful. I suppose that's the most important thing to remember. When I hear these reports—it reminds me...you have to think like a criminal—and most people don't."

CHAPTER TWENTY-TWO

Charlotte

I t's highly probable that this time tomorrow, I will be dead. That means, if I'm lucky, I have twenty-four hours left to accomplish an entire lifetime of work. This is why I'm camped out on Hayley's floor watching her sleep, plotting my next move. Turns out, there's a lot to think about when considering the end of your life. It's like packing for a faraway vacation, just one you don't return from.

I always knew this was in the realm of possibilities for me. I just didn't think it would happen so soon. But then, no one does. Death usually sneaks up on you that way.

Within the past six years alone, the agency I work for has lost eight agents, five of them not to attrition. They were inside jobs. I know.

I handled three of them.

This gig is not a zero-sum game, nor is it a fair one. That's not the way the world works, no matter what people want to believe.

This is the problem with society. If the average person knew that what are likely my very last hours walking the earth will be spent on scum like Geoffrey Dunsmore, instead of my family, they'd say I was the crazy one. It's obviously no secret that most people are fucking idiots.

But still. I do not like to leave things unfinished. And, sure, I'll admit it. It's a little bit of a personal vendetta. If it had not been for Geoffrey Dunsmore bringing his prey onto my flight, I never would have been in that grocery store in the first place, and then none of this would have ever happened.

My life would not have unraveled. I would not have been exposed.

Even without extreme time constraints, when handling a job, there is a lot of room for error. It isn't like you see in the movies. Sometimes you don't get the kill. Not right off. Even if you have an entire lifetime, which after the latest series of events in my life, it is pretty clear I no longer have.

That's what I've been thinking about for hours tonight as I moved back and forth between the girls' rooms, staring at them as they sleep. I don't like to think that this is the last time I'll ever see them, but the reality of the situation—the nature of my work— has always meant that each trip very well could be.

I picture them as babies, the endless nights, almost like this one. I imagine them as toddlers, the days that once felt like they'd last forever, now long gone. And while I feel something akin to sadness, more than anything, I feel incredibly grateful that I've gotten this long.

I never wanted to be a mother. But then Sophie was born, and I was surprised to find that I didn't hate it. It wasn't instant. I never quite got the overwhelming feeling I've heard other mothers describe. I didn't think that she was something I couldn't live without. But the fierce protectiveness, the desire to see her excel in life, that was always there.

My phone vibrates next to me, a reminder that another video

has cropped up. More girls being held against their will. More girls being traded and sold like animals. More girls being raped. More girls dying. Balancing my laptop on my knee, I power it on, lower the brightness, and slip my ear buds in.

The video begins with a shot of an empty bedroom. There's a twin bed and a lounge chair, a dresser and matching nightstand. The comforter is pink, the pillowcase trimmed in lace. It is evident I am looking at a child's bedroom. The camera moves shakily, panning outward, and then there is only darkness. When the image comes into focus again, it moves swiftly through a bush. A bedroom window appears. The camera pans backward and zooms out as a girl dressed in her underwear comes into view. She is naked from the waist up. A blue towel is wrapped around her head.

The room fills with soft light as she switches on a lamp on the nightstand. There's a painting of a white horse on the wall and a book on the foot of the bed.

The camera pans in as she drops the towel. She seems to consider something for a moment and then moves to pick it up. She lays it over the lounge chair in the corner. Closer to the light, I can see that her underwear are purple, her breasts nonexistent. Sandy blonde hair, long angular face. She can't be more than eleven.

The camera moves slowly backward as a tree limb moves in front of the lens. When the bedroom comes into focus again, there is a man at the window. The girl stands with her back to him, arms folded across her chest. He approaches the girl and then peers out into the darkness, smiles, and as satisfaction passes over his features, he closes the curtains. It's Geoffrey Dunsmore. He is aware they are being watched, and he welcomes it.

I AM NOT NAIVE ENOUGH TO THINK THAT KILLING DUNSMORE, OR

any other pedophile for that matter, will put an end to videos like the one I've just watched. But that has never been the point. There is only one thing that can combat evil, and it isn't what most people think.

If I don't kill again, and *soon*, I am going to further spiral down this rabbit hole I've slipped into. I am going to keep giving interviews, keep training strangers on the internet, and I'm going to put my family further at risk.

I don't know if it surprises me or not that I am like my own mother in that way, someone who could so easily trade this life, this family, for another, effortlessly, the way you might sub out a ham sandwich for turkey.

I suppose it's in my DNA. My father understood this every time he suited up for work, every time he walked out the door. It was there in his eyes, the sorrow of doing something he loved, knowing the risk of losing us, weighing the two each time he put on his badge.

And ultimately, it was not a fair fight. Two months before Sophie was born, my father was killed in the line of duty. It wasn't a dramatic thing—he was dispatched to a local bar to break up a fight. A drunk swung a Maglite at someone, striking my father in the process, fracturing his skull in three places. In the hospital, though unconscious, he looked like himself. Peaceful and perhaps slightly amused, his expression was fixed.

Hours turned into days. As I stroked his weathered hand, he smelled of the beer and trash he'd landed in. Even though I washed him, just like the nurse had showed me, that smell, so unlike my father, never went away. Eight days in, he died from a brain bleed.

It was a relief to leave that hospital room, that smell, that fixed expression. But from that moment on, everything was different. Everything that I'd ever belonged to, or that had belonged to me, was either dead or gone. Everything except the baby I was carrying and the stranger I'd agreed to marry.

CHAPTER TWENTY-THREE

JC

My heart thumps so fast it robs me of breath. What irony this is, I think, as I listen to the footsteps coming from behind, counting them as they hit the pavement. I am following her. He is following me.

Memorizing the rhythm of his footsteps, I listen as one by one they match mine. Judging by the thud with which they hit the ground, I know he has picked up pace. I know he is close.

Why this man is following me, I haven't a clue. In any case, at 1:44 in the morning, when you're in a dark, empty park on the edge of town, *why* becomes irrelevant, because whatever the reason, it can't be good.

This is not how this is supposed to go, I muse, tightening my grip around the base of the knife. I steady my breath, and as I run the coolness of the blade across my fingertip, I audibly exhale. On my next inhale, I mentally prepare myself for a possible confrontation, and then I slow my pace and wait.

He, too, slows, before he switches up his pace. With each step forward, I sense him there, lurking in the shadows not far behind, and the thought of us coming face to face does not exactly thrill me.

I can feel he's holding back and so I stop abruptly and turn— certain if I spun around to my left I could reach out and touch him. Only when I do, there's no one behind me. Or at least, not that I can see.

He's there, I'm certain. Although I can't see anything, nothing further than a few inches in front of my face, I can feel his body heat.

A dead silence fills the air, and even when I strain to make sense of my surroundings, I don't hear anything except the intermittent rush of wind.

For a second, I'm annoyed with his reluctance to show himself. I imagine us facing off, a scenario which ends with me subsequently snapping his neck. Not only is he rudely interrupting my sleep, he's being sloppy about it as well. He shouldn't be here—he shouldn't be involved with her. He shouldn't be following me.

Taking a step backward, I scan the dark edges of the wooded area just beyond the point where the soft glow of the lamp posts touch.

Carefully, I begin to turn and start back the way I came. I figure if he won't show himself, then I'll retreat to the warmth and the safety of my truck and wait him out. I take just two steps before I feel him closing in. I firmly adjust the base of the knife in my palm, strengthening my grip, and suddenly, his hands are on me. With one hand clasped against my mouth, the other around my shoulders, he drags me backward into a row of thick bushes.

This isn't even remotely how this night was supposed to go, I think, bucking against him, utilizing all of my bodyweight as I attempt to ram my foot into his shin. Unfortunately, he's quick. He dodges it, and I don't make any headway at getting free. Bringing the knife around my body, where I plan to plunge it into the arm he has draped around my neck, I stab at the air, missing the chance. In the scuffle, we move sideways, out of the brush and onto the path, where he releases me and backs away.

It takes milliseconds for my brain to fully register what I am seeing, but in the dark, the shiny metal of the revolver pointed at my head is unmistakable.

I hold my hands palm up. "Easy," I say, my eyes adjusting to the light of the lamppost. I can hardly make out his face, much less his features, but I can easily hear his breathing. He isn't panicked. His hand is steady.

"Whatever you want, take it," I say to him, but I know I am going to die.

"You," he says, shining a flashlight at my face, blinding me. "You put cameras in her home." He widens his stance and steadies his gun. "You sick bastard."

I fling myself to the side as he fires the gun, and then I take off in a full sprint in the opposite direction. Sound travels fast in the cold, and the sound I hear is a relief, a thousand prayers answered. The pistol misfires.

My legs burn, the undergrowth tears at my pants, but I press onward. Gasping for air, I fill my lungs, trying to maximize the oxygen in my bloodstream. It will help to outrun him.

But it is not enough. I feel him gaining ground. I can tell by the way the hairs on the back of my neck stand on end. Suddenly, I feel everything—from the moonless sky to the thickness of my breath in the air, I feel it all. The darkness that surrounds us is chilling, and I feel that too, and then he is on me, taking me to the ground. I don't fight him on the way down. I don't resist. Instead, I work within his swift movements.

Using my fingers to make out the contours of the hardened muscles of his upper thigh, I once again steady the knife in my grip and take a breath in. On the exhale, I plunge the blade into what I hope to be his femoral artery. It's dark, so I pull the knife back, feeling it graze bone. Deftly, I plunge it in once more. He staggers forward and then onto his knees, before toppling heavily to the ground. When the movement ceases, I know I have made the right cut, and finally, I no longer hear his labored breath.

It's then that something else catches my attention— the shuffling of gravel, the unmistakable sound of footsteps, coming up the path.

I make a start toward the nearest set of bushes, ducking behind them. Doubling over, I rest my palms on my thighs and try to be silent. My fingers and toes buzz, and my chest is throbbing, silently pleading for a giant racking sob of inhalation.

"Henry?" she says, quietly. "Henry! Oh my God."

CHAPTER TWENTY-FOUR

Charlotte

Looking at my reflection in the tiny bathroom mirror on the plane, I am unrecognizable. This time it isn't the hair or the makeup or the uniform. It's in the eyes, although it has nothing to do with the colored contacts I'm wearing.

Wiping tears away, I carefully dab at my eyelids, worried that I will undo all of the effort I just put in. My mascara is sure to run.

Dabbing a little concealer under my lids, I check my appearance once more.

In this line of work, it is always important to remind yourself who the enemy is. To keep it in the forefront of your mind and to drill it way down deep, so that when the time comes there is little doubt, there is no backing out.

But this time...well... this time the enemy is myself.

Henry is dead. I very well should be. Whoever killed him was also targeting me, but I was late, and for whatever reason, inevitably spared. I could feel eyes on me; it was clear I was being watched. Henry had set the rendezvous to make the drop, details and instructions for the hit on Dunsmore, which I was able to retrieve from him, after he'd bled out in the dirt. Often, he kept a tiny slip of paper taped to the bottom of his watch. This time, it was in the inside of his shoe. When I'd asked him to email the info he'd refused, saying there was something he wanted to discuss with me, and I got the impression that it was important, the kind of information he wouldn't want the agency or anyone else to get their hands on.

For obvious reasons, I was concerned it was a trap— that Henry had lured me to that park, that I had become his mark—so I hung back and waited him out, which is why I was late.

Whoever was there intended to kill us both. It hit me, in that park—I could not go home. Not then, not ever again. To do so would be certain death for my family. They will be watching the house. Hence the tears. The best thing I can do now would be to get as far away as possible and wait for word from the agency. Their next move could come in the form of a bullet or in the form of information.

Until then, I have to carry out my current assignment as scheduled, and carry on as normal. Or at least pretend. Fifteen good years I have given the agency. Numerous kills. *An ungodly number of kills.* Now, it's me they want. First, they got Henry.

Henry was the closest thing to a real friend that I've ever had. It's my fault he is dead. He came to warn me, to help me, and I let him die.

It is just a matter of time before they will find me, and they will kill me. My death will be explained away easily, a tragic accident that took place during a work trip. If my family is spared, the insurance money should serve them well.

My chin quivers as more tears threaten to spill over. I am thankful that I never confided in Michael. It was the best decision I ever made. Each and every lie. All these years, so many times I could have easily slipped. I never did. And for that I am proud.

Speaking of pride, I check my reflection once more, and I think about what I want to leave behind, about the things I need to make amends for, and about finishing what I started.

MEN LIKE GEOFFREY DUNSMORE AREN'T EASY TO GET ALONE. NOT that I have to have him alone. At this point, I suppose it doesn't matter. But it does make it easier.

Flying to Paris without Henry, although wonderfully quiet and almost peaceful, feels sad and wrong. The interior of the jet is pleasantly empty, and I sink into my seat, exhausted. Takeoff is delayed, and dusk has fallen by the time the aircraft finally lifts its wheels, banks over the glittering city, and sets its course for Paris.

France always conjures memories of Dan the pilot. It's where we first met, it's where we first fucked, and if my calculations are correct, it's where Sophie was conceived.

It also happens to be where I killed him.

I hadn't meant for it to happen. Not really. Poor Dan. He had somewhat of a choking fetish. He liked it if I pressed and held his carotid artery just enough to bring him to the brink, right to the edge of consciousness. He liked leather; he liked to be tied up. He enjoyed putting himself in dangerous situations, and I was always more than eager to help.

There was no variance with Dan. He was well known among our colleagues for his dalliances, his incessant one-night stands. Sometimes, as it happened with me, Dan picked a regular and hung onto them, until the shine wore off, or in my case, until I became a liability.

There were no shortage of warnings that came my way. Sometimes they came in the form of stories, other times in glances of pity. I was determined to prove everyone wrong.

That trip, the one right before our final flight, after we engaged in his rather ritualistic manner of sex, we laid side by side in Dan's hotel room. Talking about the future—or rather Dan talked, and I listened. He hadn't meant to let it slip, but he had. He wasn't flying back to the States with me and the crew. He wouldn't be in the U.S. when the abortion was scheduled, or even reachable by phone, but he said I could email, if I wanted. He explained that he was off to Italy, on an anniversary trip with his wife. His kids were scheduled to meet them partway through, as an extended vacation was planned to celebrate his daughter's graduation. As he discussed the logistics, there was something in the way he said it that made me realize I wasn't in his future. I was just a diversion along the way to it.

AT THE AIRPORT, I WEAVE IN AND OUT OF WEARY PASSENGERS, taking care to watch for surveillance. The best way to notice if you're being followed is to keep moving. Following a person is really more of an art rather than a science, and surveillance trade-craft is no exception. Like playing the violin or running a marathon, it takes time and practice to become a skilled surveillance practitioner. Lucky for me, most people involved in tradecraft simply do not devote the time necessary to master this skill. Because of this, they have terrible technique, use sloppy procedures, and lack finesse when they are tailing people.

Henry taught me best. Surveillance is actually an unnatural activity, and a person partaking in it must deal with strong feel-ings of self-consciousness and of being out of place. People conducting surveillance frequently suffer from what is called "burn syndrome," the erroneous belief that the people they are watching have spotted them. Feeling "burned" will cause surveil-lants to do unnatural things, such as suddenly ducking back into a doorway or turning around abruptly when they unexpectedly come face to face with the target. People inexperienced in the art of surveillance find it difficult to control this natural reaction.

Even those of us who are experienced surveillance operatives occasionally have the feeling of being burned; the difference is we have received a lot of training and are better able to control our reaction and work through it. The most important thing is to maintain a normal-looking demeanor, even when your insides are screaming that the person you are surveilling has seen you.

The more I am able to stop and pause and survey my surroundings, the easier it will be to spot surveillance. So, I enter the airport bathroom and freshen up, adding thick-rimmed glasses to my repertoire.

I fix the blonde wig in place, rearrange several errant pieces of hair, and, finally satisfied, I smile at my handiwork. Given how far from my natural color I have gone, I am surprised I don't look half bad. When my expression softens, once again going slack, I look weary and useless, and ultimately very ordinary, which just might help.

I don't resemble Charlotte Jones in the least.

Instead of taking a shuttle to the hotel, I hail a taxi. In a cab, it will be easier to spot if I'm being followed. I can give the driver instructions, change directions, direct him where I want him to go if I need to lose a tail.

The driver glares at me in the rearview in a way that makes me uneasy. Even though the flight across the Atlantic is official, a real job, transporting a real businessman, and the agency wants to see this job carried out, one can never be too cautious. So I pat the handgun in my luggage, a reminder that all can be equal should I need it to be.

He speaks in broken French into a cell phone, and I make out that he is having an argument with his son.

Turning my attention toward the window, I glare out at the city of light. I've always hated Paris, but I hate it more in the winter. Maybe I hate it more because it's the kind of place one is supposed to love. I feel nothing of the sort. There are too many people and not a single reason to feel alone.

Tonight, the last thing I want is to be alone. I am on a mission, and that mission, and being in Paris, makes me want to go dancing. And so I do.

I meet her on the dance floor, soft and sweaty, about five minutes past her prime. Dark hair, watchful eyes. She speaks only French. Me, hardly any. She is my contact. She knows things I need to know. The rest I forget. It won't matter tomorrow anyhow.

Or later in my hotel room, either.

THE ATMOSPHERE IN THE BEDROOM IS HEAVY, WITH A HINT OF lavender in the air. The pale carpet beneath my feet is soft and thick.

Now that we are here in my hotel room, everything feels a little more serious; the sexuality I had tossed around freely at the nightclub feels suddenly dangerous. Nothing in life is free, information included.

The physical act is easy enough, mostly mechanical when it comes right down to it. Kissing. Fingers. Oral and manual stimulation. It's all acting, really. So what if sometimes you enjoy the job? Still, I wonder what I would lose if I seduced this woman. Nothing, I realize. There is nothing that could be taken from me that hasn't already been taken.

Afterward, naked, she perches herself on a chair, like a lazy house cat, and smokes a cigarette. It's not a small room, I've stayed in worse. Still, she takes up too much space. She's hardly said a word, what little sex we had was awful, and I'm not sure I've ever hated anyone more. She says something in French, something universal, something along the lines of *how long are you here for? When can I see you again?*

I offer only two words in response: Geoffrey Dunsmore.

She crinkles her nose, looks momentarily surprised, before exhaling a thick plume of smoke into the air.

Another reason to hate Paris. Everyone smokes.

Slipping into the hotel robe, I walk over to where she's perched and show her his picture on my phone. She knows I know she knows him. And I know she knows how and where to locate him. The two have a relationship of sorts. "I need to find him."

She shrugs and mumbles something in French.

"Can you tell me where he hangs out?"

"This, I do not know."

I smile, walk across the room, and lay the phone on the table. I love it when people pretend not to speak your language but very obviously do. It makes things simple.

"He's a friend of a friend," I tell her. "I think he's your friend as well, no?"

"We've spent time together. Yes."

"Do you know where I can find him?"

She takes a long pull on her cigarette and then shrugs as she turns her face to the ceiling and exhales. "La Tempête, perhaps."

Dropping the robe, I walk over to her and place my hands gently on the side of her face. "Merci."

Leaning in and kissing her on the mouth, I sigh. She tastes like stale cigarettes and easy lies. "You were wonderful."

My hands cup her slender face as she takes a long drag from her cigarette. Before she gets the chance to exhale, I snap her neck.

CHAPTER TWENTY-FIVE

Charlotte

The club is everything I expected. When you've seen one of its kind, you've pretty much seen them all. The decor is black velvet and gold trim, the synthesis of luxury and comfort evident in every detail. You can dance, drink, and—if your pockets are deep enough— have whatever suits your tastes. With its incredible interior, which combines antique furniture with modern atmosphere, every wall is decorated with mirrors, which make the club more interesting, especially when they distort the bodies of the people writhing on the dance floor.

It's already the wee hours of the morning by the time I arrive. I only have a few hours until daylight when the vampires who frequent these sorts of places will grow tired and take the party elsewhere, retreating to their respective covens.

The hours are weighing on me. I have a long night ahead, and I'm jet-lagged as it is.

Already I've put in a full day's work and then some. It takes a lot to get a dead body out of a hotel room. I don't know what I was thinking. We really should have gone to her place.

In order to make her fit into my oversized luggage bag, I had to break both of her legs and one of her arms. I don't know what I would have done if she hadn't been tiny. It's a small miracle she was fit and trim, even by Parisian standards.

I rolled her straight out through the lobby and into the night. As I walked along the Seine, I thought of her tongue dancing with mine, her slender fingers, her shallow smile, and I wondered who might miss her.

I called home and spoke to Michael and the girls. They were busy living their lives, bickering with each other, sending point-less instant messages. It is not enough to stop and talk to me. I am their mother, a wife—there will always be tomorrow. In their eyes I will always be a given. They have no idea this could be the last time they hear my voice. It makes me wonder who the woman in the suitcase last spoke to by phone. Was it important? Was it someone she loved? Did they make it count?

Pointless questions on my part. I tell the girls I love them and Michael too. Then I switch off the phone, and when I am sure no one is looking, I simply kick the suitcase into the murky, cold black water. No doubt the suitcase will surface in time. The autopsy will rule her death a murder, but by then, I'll be long gone.

———

GEOFFREY DUNSMORE IS NOT IN ATTENDANCE TONIGHT, BUT there's no shortage of other people to look at. There are bodies everywhere. Naked, the young and the beautiful and seemingly restless.

It takes speaking to six people before I have an address in hand.

As I finish off my glass of white wine, searching the address on my phone, I glance up every once in a while, pausing to watch the patrons partake in various forms of sex. So far as I can tell, there's no rhyme or reason to why two or more people partner up, and given the right mood, it might turn me on. Might even make me a little homesick, all the writhing, sweaty, eager bodies. It's too bad none of them are the one I want.

LISTENING FOR THE CLICK OF THE LOCK, MY EYES TAKE A SECOND TO adjust as soft light floods the room. I can just make out two shadows through the crack I have left, so I slide the door open just a little more. This time, it's my turn to watch.

Dunsmore turns to the girl and drapes his arm over her shoulders. He kisses her once lightly on the mouth and runs his hand across her cheek. Then he pulls her closer and kisses her roughly.

Dunsmore pulls away and looks at her through heavy-lidded eyes. Pure desire, barely contained.

The girl is young, but not as young as the ones in the video. This one may even be of age, but not by much. My body tenses, a thousand nerves exposed. The feeling in my stomach is sick, rolling like the ocean during a storm.

Through the doors of the armoire, I watch as he shrugs his jacket to the floor and starts for the buttons on his shirt. I have been hidden, wedged in here for hours now, my bladder painfully full, my head dizzy from stale air and a lack of oxygen.

Leaning forward, I see the girl come into focus. She reaches behind her and unzips her dress, making it clear that this is not her first dance with Geoffrey Dunsmore. It is evident in her eyes. She is aware of her allure. She takes up the space she inhabits confidently. She has learned how to use her body; the question is whether or not she really wants to, how much of this is an act.

Freed of the dress, the girl plops backward onto the bed, propped by her elbows, naked except for a pair of panties.

Dunsmore walks slowly toward her, takes her leg by the ankle, and pulls her to the edge of the bed. He pops her foot into his mouth and sucks on her big toe before slowly moving his lips over the rest of her foot, swirling his tongue along the arch, nestling his face in it.

This goes on forever, as my bladder screams at me, until finally, he places the girl's bent leg on the bed with a pat, and slithers toward the headboard like the snake he is. He is eager, his mouth hard at work, until he reaches the utmost point of her inner thigh. I register the sound, the tearing of panties, the rhythmic sound of the mattress.

As the rocking grows louder, erratic, and less predictable, I know this is my chance. Moving in time with Dunsmore's grunting, I push the armoire door forward and slowly climb out.

He is on top of the girl, pumping away. I tiptoe across the room. The huffing grows as he moves harder and faster. Apart from the pale yellow glow flickering across the room, the moaning and skin slapping, I am surprised that I feel calm and in control.

Dunsmore's naked backside comes into focus as I wrap the wire tightly around my fists. I lunge forward onto the bed, cat-like, and, kneeling over him, I place the steel wire across his throat. It sounds like percussion as I draw it tight, cutting into his flesh. He bucks against my legs, flapping like a fish out of water as his hands scramble for his throat. I can feel him tugging, pulling at the wire, although he is unable to make any headway, because the more he struggles, the tighter I pull.

With a yank upward, the steel wire brushes his windpipe, and I feel a slight give in his flesh. My eyes meet the girl's. She stares uncomprehendingly up at me, her mouth open.

His fingers move as though he is playing a frantic piano tune, desperately trying to get a fix on the wire. In time, his body begins to convulse, shaking violently like a puppy attempting to shake a lead.

The girl begins to push at his chest, writhing to break free, hopelessly trying to avoid the blood that is raining down on her. Blood from Dunsmore's severed neck paints the girl's face, chest, and hands. Even as the convulsing begins to ebb and wane, the gurgling continues.

I do not let up on the wire, allowing it to move through his flesh, through his windpipe, severing his neck to the extent that my upper body strength will allow.

Geoffrey Dunsmore is not a small man. My arms ache, my throat burns, breathing is shallow and comes rapidly.

When the tremors start, I cannot be sure whether they are his or mine, but eventually his body sputters like an old car running out of gas, and then the whole room goes still.

For a full minute, the girl stares at me before she moves to the far corner of the bed, covering herself, cowering in the corner like a frightened animal.

I climb over the corpse, search for his arm, his wrist tucked carefully under his giant belly. It takes some effort, but I manage to wriggle it free. Quickly, I remove his watch. The girl begins to cry, producing massive racking sobs. Only when I hold it up, does she pause. "A Rolex, of course," I say, and then I smile, thinking Henry would be proud.

CHAPTER TWENTY-SIX

JC

It's been a pretty rough twenty-four hours. First, I followed her to France, where I learned that not only does she have a penchant for sex clubs, she has a thing for old men. Disappointing, to say the least.

This is why you can't leave people to their own vices.

This was apparent as I watched her in Paris, from a vantage point directly across the street. She wore a short blonde wig and heavy eye makeup covered by thick-rimmed glasses, making it obvious she didn't want to be recognized.

The wig fell pleasantly around her face, and a heavy frown played across her face. She fidgeted often, alluding to a sense of nervousness that could only be explained by being in a foreign country, alone, at night.

She is the kind of woman who can't bear to be on her own, something I find suitable to my tastes. This knowledge manifested as I watched her pick up a woman on the dance floor and take her back to her room. She's full of surprises, this one. I wanted to be inside that hotel room, I wanted to see what she was like when she was undressed, when she made love, when she thought no one was looking.

I'd grown accustomed to this privilege, and there on that street corner in the cold and drizzle, I couldn't help but feel cheated.

I waited a long while on that corner, standing in the dark, before I gave up. Fearing I might be noticed, I retreated to my room, stopping first at the front desk, where I paid the night attendant to text me if and when Charlotte left her room.

Women are so willing to sell other women out. She has no idea. This is why she needs me. This is why she needs to be careful. People will do almost anything for a buck.

I don't know if I was surprised or not when the text came through. Watching her stroll along the banks of the Seine, I worried for her safety. She brought along her suitcase, which didn't help her cause. She looked like a tourist. She was distracted, with her nose in her phone. I was concerned that she might have decided to head back early, but then she kicked the suitcase into the water, and I realized I had a lot more to worry about than being left behind.

What are you up to, Charlotte? I thought as I watched her enter that seedy club. Seeing her there, seeing her in that context, caused something in me to shift. She is a wife and a mother, but she is acting like a whore. I felt an anger building. Perhaps there was the sense of injustice, a level of disappointment I was coming to understand. Maybe she can't be what I want her to be. Maybe she can't be what *anyone* wants her to be.

All I know is, there is only one way to find out.

CAN SHE SENSE THAT THINGS ARE ABOUT TO CHANGE—THAT LIFE AS she knows it hangs precariously in the balance? Can she feel my eyes on her? Does she have a sixth sense when it comes to monsters? Thinking about it makes me happy. Perversely, there is a part of me that hopes she does possess an extra sense for detecting evil. But I've been watching her for weeks; I know she is completely oblivious to my presence. Even when she is aware that I exist in the same space, she stays fixed in her own world, easily banishing me to its outskirts.

From France, she stewarded my return flight to Dallas, on which she spoke a total of eight words to me. She has to be the worst flight attendant in history. Of the three businessmen and me, everyone said it, at least once.

It's hard to be good at your job when you've spent so much time on nefarious distractions. I'm worried about her. She looks sickly, her face gaunt and pale, truth be told. With heavy bags and dark circles under her eyes, it's blatantly clear—the nightlife is not for her.

Once the passengers deplaned and we refueled, she was scheduled for my chartered flight to Anchorage. After a brief layover, and a change of crew, we set course for Alaska.

Now, it is just the two of us. Exactly as it should be.

You really have no idea what it takes to get her alone.

The pilots are with her too.

Although, they don't count. They're dead.

So, it's just me up here in the cockpit. Me and a dispensary of half-empty pill bottles. Xanax, Valium, codeine, Adderall—pretty much anything you could want— I have it all lined up in a neat little row on top of the instrument panel.

Maybe it's worth mentioning, I'm not usually this laid back. Second thing you should know, I don't typically fly while under the influence, but this is what you could call a special circumstance.

Up here, where the air is thin, there's just us trying to stay above the weather.

Well, at least one of us is trying.

The other one is all sad-eyed and what you could call emotional. Could be the zip ties. It's not the first time I've been accused of taking things too far.

That and *well...* she doesn't particularly care for the term "hostage." Obviously, this is more than that. If anyone has been the captive in this whole ordeal, it's me. Could be, too, that she's thinking about her children. They'll be fine. I did my best to assure her. They're old enough to make their own food, tie their own shoes. They have a spare parent. Not everyone is so lucky, I said. Not everyone gets to have two.

She didn't seem comforted by this, but then, she's always had a bit of a poker face.

Maybe the two of us are more alike than we are different.

Originally, my plan was to take us down over the Pacific.

A suicide mission with an unwilling and unsuspecting victim.

But the better I feel, the more the pills kick in and work their magic, the more I see the possibility in a shitty situation. It makes me think I'm not yet ready for this fantasy to end.

CHAPTER TWENTY-SEVEN

Charlotte

I wake with a headache that feels like my head has been split in two. Right away, I notice several things at once: it is dark, my breathing is labored and shallow, and in a terrible twist of irony, I am folded in an impossible position and wedged into a very small space. Am I moving? My vision is hazy, my eyes open and close rapidly, out of instinct, to gain a semblance of balance, recognition of anything I can use as information. Knowledge is power, and I know this from SERE training: Survival, Evasion, Resistance, Escape. In this situation, every bit of information counts.

What I know is I am in a moving vehicle. Ripped vinyl tears at my back, a sensation made worse with each bump and groove in the road. My hands are still tied behind my back, just as they had been on the plane. My ankles are bound by duct tape and my legs are decidedly very heavy.

Flexing my feet back and forth, I wiggle my toes, trying to get blood flowing. Any attempt at an escape is going to require running. Having the use of my legs is not optional. It is imperative.

My first instinct is to fight. It's a battle between what my brain and my body is telling me to do. That's what you do when your worst nightmare is playing out in front of you. It takes everything in me to metaphorically step back and evaluate the situation. For the most part, this is an involuntary response, perfected over millenniums, a flood of chemicals that contribute to the flight or fight mechanism hardwired into our brains. My training reinforced that, teaching me how to override it.

Taking a deep breath in, I hold it. Then let it out. I repeat the process over and over until I'm lightheaded but almost calm. I remind myself that half the battle is in waiting for a time to escape that maximizes my chance of being successful. Most captives do not get the chance to escape twice.

My nervous system will assist me, I know from SERE, but overriding my sense of fear is critical. It will be a hindrance. Physical skills will be worthless if I'm so frozen or paralyzed by the psychological and mental aspects of events going on around me that I am helpless.

As my breathing steadies, I think back on what I know about escape. Awareness and attitude are at their peak for the first 24-72 hours. Before captors have introduced any sort of routine. This is, of course, if they plan to keep you alive. Fact is, most of the time they don't.

I have to use this initial time to my advantage. In any abduction, the best chance of escape happens while your captors are on the move and during that initial two to three days.

I tell myself this, force myself to think about these things, but all of this knowledge, this training, means nothing now. Not until it happens can you really know what to do and how to act. Until the training is put into action, it's just information. And what they don't tell you, what you can't know, is how the fear settles deep in your bones, embedding itself in every fiber of your being. This has always been the worst of all my fears, being detained and tortured until I'm ultimately killed. I'd been careful to avoid it. I followed the rules in terms of becoming invisible. I've kept my head down. I changed my appearance, I took what I thought were calculated risks. And still, my worst nightmare has found me. I can hear my father's voice in my head, asking me, "What now?"

I drift in and out of sleep. The truck rocks along slowly. I am slung haphazardly over the seat in the small cab. I know I have been drugged. My head swims and bounces across the worn vinyl seat heavily. I don't think I could lift it if I tried.

Several times I turn my head to the side and vomit, the side of my face moist, my throat and neck covered in it.

I think I hear music on the radio, gravel crunching under the tires, as they move along the road. Sometimes there's a sharp buzzing sound, and other times, it's Henry's voice I hear. As my eyes flutter, open and closed, I see him there, sitting next to me, even though I know this is impossible. Henry is dead. But when I drift, it feels real, the warmth of his lap and my head resting against his thigh. Occasionally, he leans down and whispers something in my ear. He rattles the information off in Henry's way. He does not try to comfort me, he only lists the instructions off methodically, and while I know it is a dream, that it isn't real, somewhere deep in the pit of me a sob escapes. I want to believe.

Keep your attitude strong internally, but, Liv, whatever you do, do not show this to your captor. Instead, show physical signs of surrender or submission. Remember: it's all an act. Head down, shoulders hunched forward, walk in a shuffle, acquiring a slight limp or feigning injury, illness, or weakness. Speak low and softly. Address your captors with a conveyed fear and respect. Cry. Act as though you've given up. This is how you give yourself some advantage.

Role play your weaknesses. Develop a fictional "story" for yourself around it. This will not only help you stay in character, it will give you a fake "breaking point" (a point where you break down and pretend to be emotionally destroyed, as though you've completely given up), if you are being tortured or hurt for information or amusement by your captors. Think about your family, think about them being in your position, imagine witnessing something so horrible happening to your children that you can't get over it. Whatever it takes, do it. It's your only shot at survival.

And remember all the things we went over. Force yourself to recall your training, our hours upon hours in the air, discussing cases like what you are facing.

You are an attractive woman, Olivia. You must work to make yourself less attractive. Use dirt and filth, fake your period, illness, change your posture, and set your face with an uninviting scowl. But make sure you understand your captor first. You do not want to end up as a throwaway captive, if you could have used your sexuality to your advantage.

You need to buy yourself enough time and opportunity to escape, and in the meantime, you need to do whatever it takes to survive and remain healthy up to that point. The sooner that opportunity comes, the better your chance of survival, if you do manage an escape.

Try not to stand out in any way. Playing a weak and submissive person affords you the element of surprise if you do have to overcome your captors. It makes you less of a threat. They will grow lax; they will not watch you as closely.

Most binds can be fairly easily removed and worn down with any rough edge or friction. Getting out of restraints is not as difficult as it will seem. Most material stretches.

But most importantly, don't forget to remain aware. Mimic the way a cat steps outside. Stop and smell the air, listen and watch. Slowly transition. Not only will this provide you information about your surroundings, it will make you seem weak and fearful.

THE NEXT TIME I WAKE, LARGE HANDS DIG INTO MY UNDERARMS while my legs, outstretched, flop along haphazardly. I am being dragged across a hard floor, assumingly toward the running water

I hear. Or maybe that's just my mind playing tricks. The pounding in my head drums incessantly, making it difficult to tell what is real. I don't want to open my eyes to find out.

I have to.

The room spins, the world as I know it shifts and tilts, and without warning, I vomit. He drops me, and I roll onto my side. My face welcomes the feel of the cool tile, as I lay there dry heaving, the man stands above me, his hands on his hips, making it clear this is not what he expected. I look up at him, my expression pleading. "We have to get you feeling better," he says, just before I close my eyes, lay my head next to my vomit, and pass out again.

———

SOMETIME LATER WHEN I REGAIN CONSCIOUSNESS, I AM IN A DIMLY lit room, tied to a bed. Tears flood my eyes, and a whimper escapes my lips.

It comes to me in flashes, each time I fade in and out. This time is no different. The gun. Waking up on the plane, zip tied and thoroughly restrained. The dead men in the seats next to me, staring blankly ahead. Tires on a gravel road. Ripped vinyl. The sour smell of vomit. The cold shower. The softly spoken words. The smell of sandalwood.

Tethered at my wrists and ankles to the frame, my restraints have some give, thankfully, but when I shift, a burning sensation floods my senses. There is nowhere I do not feel it. My hair is wet, my neck is stiff, and worse, when I attempt to turn my head, I discover I can't. I'm wearing some sort of neck brace.

Of what I can see, the room is spacious and well decorated, the kind of place that feels homey. It doesn't look remote, or unkempt, but rather the kind of place that someone might visit or find, which gives me hope. Considering hope, I go through the list of things I know. I assume that I am somewhere in Alaska, as that is where we were headed, considering there was a flight plan. Still,

I have no idea where in Alaska, if that is even correct, nor how long I have been asleep. We could be anywhere. What I do know is that the walls around me are made of logs. I am in a bedroom.

I sense that I am being watched. Somewhere close, but not too close, I hear the faint sound of music. Opera. I smell fire, burning wood and smoke, cinnamon and food cooking.

Aside from the neck contraption, I am wearing wool pajamas that I obviously did not put on myself. My lips are bone dry, my tongue heavy in my mouth. My eyes want desperately to close. My mind beckons sleep. It's my only escape.

But knowing I can't prolong the inevitable; I do what must be done. I struggle, loudly, so as to let him know that I am awake. Better to get this over with, I tell myself, even if my insides are screaming it is a terrible mistake.

HE MOVES SLOWLY INTO THE ROOM. "OH, GOOD. YOU'RE AWAKE. You had me worried there for a minute."

I can see him only partially, from the corner of my eye. But I can feel him. His strong presence, his determined energy. "Here," he says, shifting the brace on my neck, which allows me to have a little more movement. "This should help."

He takes a roll of duct tape off an antique table and tears a piece off with his teeth. Walking over to the bed, he places it gently over my mouth, despite the fact that I refuse to keep my face still. "You could scream all you want but no one would hear you. That's not the purpose of the tape, in case you're wondering. I just don't want to get bit. At least not until we've become better acquainted." He smiles. "I'm sure you understand."

I watch as he unfastens his belt and holds it in his closed fist. "You have no idea how long I've wanted this—how patient I've been."

I fight against the restraints. At least initially. He picks up scissors and holds them close to my face. "I really hope you aren't going to make this difficult."

Opening the scissors, he cuts my pajama pants from one end to the other. My breath comes faster now. No matter how much one wants to hide fear, it takes more control than you realize you are able to summon.

"Shame," he says. "I really should have thought this through." He can't remove my pants without undoing the restraints, hence the scissors.

"It's okay," he tells me, holding up the torn pants. "There's more where that came from." He smiles and then leans in and kisses the tip of my nose. "Please don't make me dose you again."

My fingers and toes clench and then flex and soften, clench and soften. "Trust me," he whispers, smoothing my hair away from my face. "You're going to want to be awake for this."

He lifts my top. My bra has been removed. He kisses my breasts, hungrily, before slowing and taking one nipple in his mouth. After swirling his tongue around it several times, he bites hard. Then he looks up at me and smiles. Tears prick the corner of my eyes. He cups both breasts and squeezes. "God. If you only knew how long I've wanted to do that."

He moves his hands slowly down my body, caressing, prodding, offering commentary along the way, saying he's getting to know the lay of the land. "You're so beautiful."

He fumbles between my legs, which makes me think he's inexperienced, until I realize he's testing me, trying to find my breaking point. "I have so many things I want to ask you, Charlotte. So many. Thankfully, there is time." He dips one finger inside me, and that does it—he has found the point he was searching for. My hips buck wildly. I realize it's pointless. Tied to this bed, all of the bucking in the world is not going to set me free or stop what is about to happen. At some point, the course was set, and the momentum has carried me here. His will is obviously strong. "Tell me…how many people have you seduced and then killed?"

He slips another finger in. "This many?"

I bite my lip until I taste blood. I count the lines in the ceiling. He adds another finger. "This many?"

When he laughs, I understand, the worst is yet to come. He is a professional. He's given this moment a lot more thought than I ever have. He has the home field advantage.

"You should know, Charlotte," he whispers, as he hovers over me. "What goes around comes around."

I quiz myself on the capital of each state. He parts my thighs and enters me. As he pumps away, I go through them alphabetically, getting all the way to Vermont. *Montpelier.* It goes against every fiber of my being and all of the training I have had. But I will not give him what he wants. I will not show fear.

CHAPTER TWENTY-EIGHT

JC

It happened quite by accident. Said another way: I didn't mean to see it. To put it nicely, she is a difficult captive, and I guess you could say, there's a part of me that was curious. I had to know. *Did I do the right thing? Did I choose well?* I don't know if it's the same for women, but all men think this way.

The term 'trophy wife' exists for a reason.

Selection is important.

Is she out of my league? But not so much that I have to worry (the last thing a man wants is his pride tested) just enough that she looks like a catch, making me look better in turn? Is she going to live up to my expectations over the long haul? Is she going to let herself go? Is she going to get fat like her mother? And if she doesn't live up to the expectations of who I need her to be—if she does get fat like her mother—how do I get rid of her with the least amount of damage?

I suppose those questions swirling around in my brain hour after hour is what leads me to check the cameras. I need to know that she is missed. I want to know that I have gained something important. I want to know how her family is holding up, and maybe, just *maybe*, if I glean a bit of information about her daughters, I can use it to my advantage, spoon feeding it to her so that she'll give me what I want.

And what is that? At this point, I have it down to a science. Believe me. What I want is for her to desire me as much as I desire her. Isn't that what everyone wants, *really*? Isn't this the very definition of love?

How rare and precious the timing of this is, I am coming to understand.

I realize that Rome wasn't built in a day. It will take sweet time to get used to one another. How much time is the question. I read the other day that it only takes four minutes to fall in love. Considering our situation is a little more challenging than your average meet-cute, I entertain the idea that it might take a bit longer than that.

In the meantime, I am keeping her comfortable. She is lucky. Luckier than she seems to realize, given her incessant tears. On one hand, the crying ignites deep and unbinding lust. It rolls through me like a throbbing tooth, the ache a strong desire to possess her, to have power over her. On the other hand, it's horrible, these never-ending, extravagant displays of emotion. The sobbing grates on my nerves, cinches my gut, makes me ill, makes me ask myself if I've made a mistake.

She has it better here than many people in third world countries. How easily she forgets. How easily I forget. It's always like this in the beginning.

Excessive displays of emotion. How funny, these days, all the fragile snowflakes, the people cry over the silliest things, the petty injustices of the world. It's easy to focus on such things when the big things, the real scary things, are not beating down your front door. How endearing it is that people think they're so safe, that they live under this false illusion that kidnappings and ransom are far-off experiences, not something that can happen close to home. It's too bad. That illusion is a facade.

Believe me, I do this for a living. Well, not a living *exactly*—that's a lie. My grandfather was an oil man, as was his grandfather's grandfather. What I do is not for the money, but for the love of the chase. For sport, you could say. A very time-consuming but rewarding hobby.

To date, I've had thirteen wives. Not legal wives, but what you might call marriages of the heart.

Training women is my specialty. It's an art, developing another human being into what you want them to be. Maybe I sound like the crazy one, but the reality is, we all do it. Some of us are simply more forceful and honest in the way we go about it, while others spend years—decades *even*—duking it out using pathetic forms of manipulation and dishonesty. That's your average marriage, anyway.

Training women is not so different than training a dog. It's difficult and unrelenting at first, but eventually, with consistency and a proper amount of communication, which is best learned in the form of reward and punishment, they, too, become eager to please.

When it works, it's almost easy. It's satisfying. When it doesn't, they die. Usually, they die. It's common to eventually get bored. My grandfather taught me that. He bred horses and later hunting dogs.

He always said: A dog's life is maybe a decade and a half if you're lucky, and then you get to start over. A marriage, on the other hand, thanks to an overabundance of fairytales, is supposed to last forever. But nothing lasts forever. Which is how it's worked out that I've endured widowhood thirteen times. It's also how Charlotte Jones came to be wife number fourteen. I think our demons could play beautifully together.

FORGIVE ME, FOR BEFORE. I WENT OFF ON A TANGENT. I MEANT TO tell you about the cameras. Never look back, my granddad always said. Solid advice. If only I'd heeded it.

If it takes four minutes for a person to fall in love; it takes less than that for everything to turn to shit.

Which is exactly what happened when I flicked on the feed to that camera. As it so happens, Mr. Jones is indeed missing his wife. He is also not who he said he was. Not in the least. It seems surprising to me that someone in his position would be oblivious to having someone not only intrude in their home but set up shop, watching his every move.

But then, if I had a nickel for every stupid move highly intelligent people made, well, I'd be rich. *Wait.* I am rich. But you get my point.

I learned two things by turning on that camera. Two very bad things.

One, Michael Jones has blood on his hands. And lots of it. Turns out, I have kidnapped a very valuable assassin. Turns out, I am a dead man walking.

I listened to him in his office. I listened as he made endless phone calls. I listened as he ranted and raged. I watched as he paced, relentlessly, at all hours. He made endless arrangements about getting his prized assassin back. He didn't speak of his wife like you might a spouse. He spoke of her like a commodity, like a product that means a lot to him. And, interestingly enough, according to his phone calls, it appears that she has no idea her husband is the one ordering her to make the hits. Something I find very hard to believe. Something I plan to get to the bottom of.

In the meantime, certain things are starting to make a lot of sense. Things that I wrote off over these last few weeks as I watched her. It turns out, Michael Jones, when not building houses, has ties to the mafia.

How nefarious, for such a meek-looking guy.

How interesting.

Although, that's not the half of it. It gets better. I noticed Mr. Jones comes and goes from his daughter's room at odd hours.

At first, I thought maybe the girl simply missed her mother. This, or maybe was helping her with her homework. I thought a lot of things. But then, I went back and searched through old footage and found the coming and going happens to be a regular occurrence when Charlotte is out of town. And then, twice, it was clear as the girl came out after him. When I zoomed in on her face, it looked exactly like her mother's. The twisted and pained expression is a familiar one. It's exactly what her mother looked like as I slid my hand between her legs.

CHAPTER TWENTY-NINE

Charlotte

When he enters my room, he brings food. Eggs and bacon, which make me want to vomit. The sight of it makes my mouth fill with saliva. The smell twists my stomach into tight knots. I have zero inclination to eat.

My nerves are on edge. My rage at being in this position is taking on a life of its own. It is an angry, living thing, gnawing and roaring along the insides of my skin.

I think of the first time I laid eyes on him, and then the second, and best of all, the third.

That was in Fort Lauderdale. I had been watching Dan's daughter. I don't know why, but on occasion, whenever we were in the same city, if I had the time, I made a hobby of searching her out and following her.

Maybe I wanted to see if Sophie was like her, if being half-sisters, they shared any characteristics. Maybe it was guilt for having taken her father away. I had learned what that was like, after all.

Anyway, people put their every move on social media, and Janine Thomas-Moore is no different. I watched her at Estero. By that point he had been stalking her for about a week. I didn't know why, but I knew enough to know that whatever the reason for his interest, it wasn't for anything good.

I recognized that kind of behavior when I saw it. It was obvious, a skill built over years of stalking and killing predators, the understanding that JC Warren was precisely that.

When everything in my life began to turn upside down, first the shooting in the grocery store, the interviews, the situation with Dunsmore, I realized that if I wanted to make a clean break, the easiest way to go about it would be to let "fate" take its course. He would not stop at my daughter's half-sister, and maybe after everything, I considered it to be paying a penance of sorts. Or maybe I was just bored and up for a challenge, off the clock. Maybe I wanted to see if I still had it in me to draw a man in. Snare him in my web. More than likely, I was thinking about how good it felt to kill a person on my own accord, pro bono, so to speak. But I won't lie. Of course, there was something in it for me. If I wanted to kill JC Warren, first I'd let him help me disappear. What a beautiful thing it is to kill so many birds with one stone.

"YOUR HUSBAND HAS QUITE THE RESUME," HE TELLS ME AS HE undresses in front of me. I assume he is speaking of architecture. It makes me sad to think of Michael and the girls, to think of them wondering where I am and why I haven't called. Have they reported me missing? I don't know. All I know is the last conversation I had with my husband was about not knowing if I wanted to stay in the marriage. Maybe it is better this way, a clean break, but when I think of my own mother and the way she left, I'm not so sure.

"I want that," he says, with a nod toward my pelvis, his expression making it clear that he has every intention of getting what he has come for. He removes the restraints from my legs. Meticulously, he massages each ankle, rubbing in careful circles. "But first...first I have something I want to discuss with you."

My eyes scan the area of the room I can see. Not much has changed; he has brought nothing with him. No phone, no weapon, nothing that could be of any use. "Here," he says, leaning in close, so that I can smell his lunch on his breath. Salmon. "Let me take this off. You're going to want the use of your head for this."

"I have to use the restroom."

He glares at me disapprovingly. "That is what the diaper is for."

"I have to use the restroom," I say once more. I don't want to seem argumentative, but I don't want to use a diaper again, either.

With a curt nod, he presses a button, and then I am being hoisted up by my bound wrists. He lifts me by my waist and shuffles me off the bed, my arms suspended above my head in the air, attached to the ceiling. He pushes another button, and I am lifted higher until I am in a standing position, painfully teetering on my tiptoes.

Hanging there on display, my body stretched out tautly, the whole of me exposed, I feel equally terrified and enraged.

He removes the adult diaper, and I watch as it falls to the floor. "I'm afraid I have some very bad news."

"What could be worse than this?" I say, unable to help myself.

"Do you really want to know?"

"Do I have a choice?"

"You always have a choice, Charlotte."

Tears sting the back of my throat as I hear my father's words in this man's mouth. Even if I chose this, it doesn't make it any easier. Sometimes we are only choosing the lesser of two evils, and I really wanted to live.

"Then I want to know."

"First—there's something I'm dying to know...why didn't you mention your occupation? Your true occupation."

I can see in his face that he is not calling my bluff. He knows who and what I am. "Would it have changed anything?"

"Probably not. But with your husband, yes. I would not have gotten close. I would have kept my distance."

"Okay?"

"What is it like working with your spouse?"

He pushes his lever again and I am pulled higher. My toes no longer graze the floor. It takes every ounce of strength I have to give him an answer, which is what he wants. "I'm not sure what you mean."

"He orders the hits, you carry them out."

I don't answer. He's not making any sense.

"Should I be worried?"

"Yes."

"I think you're right. I have captured something very valuable, Charlotte."

He walks over to me and runs his hand over the length of my torso. "Your husband is going to come looking for you, and it isn't going to be pretty, I'm afraid."

He backhands me. "You've put me in a very difficult position."

I stare at the floor, keeping my eyes fixed on one spot. The more I refuse to meet his gaze, the more submissive and defeated I will appear. He kneels and parts my thighs. "I don't think you are the kind that one just simply lets go." I feel his tongue graze me, working its way from my inner thighs to the core of me. He is not inexperienced at cunnilingus, and I find it surprising to feel my body responding to his technique.

My head lulls backward. I fix my eyes on the ceiling. If I react positively it will be over sooner and it just might earn me favor.

"How does it work, exactly? He orders the hits, you carry them out?"

My head snaps into its rightful position. "Michael is not in the business."

He stands and takes a fistful of my hair, forcing my eyes on his. "First rule, my darling. No lies."

"It's not a lie."

Releasing my head, he takes a step backward and gives me the once-over. "Do I look stupid to you?"

Before I can answer, he gut-checks me. The force of his blow knocks loose every ounce of breath I have in me. He kneels once more to kiss my stomach in the spot he hit me.

Finally, my knee connects solidly with his face. He falls back onto the floor. Incensed, he comes at me again, and this time he strikes me with a closed fist directly beneath my chin. I taste fragments of bone in my mouth, my tongue overwhelmed with the taste of blood.

"So you like to fight," he says. "I do too."

As he positions himself behind me, I spit blood onto the floor. I stare at the door, and he enters me with a brutal thrust.

Sweaty and gasping for breath, he leans forward and nibbles my ear. I clench my jaw on impulse. "Your husband is molesting your oldest daughter."

CHAPTER THIRTY

Charlotte

It is a lot to take in, the news that JC Warren delivers. Not that I need reminding, but he is a psychopath. It is in his nature, and undoubtedly it's a goal of his to unhinge me. He has certainly done that.

I tell myself it can't be true; Michael could never, he *would* never, behave inappropriately toward Sophie. At least I don't think. *Would he?*

Whether or not what JC Warren says is true, I don't know. What I do know is that his revelation makes me question my whole life. Like any mother would, I pore over the details of our daily lives, I think back on the years, searching for signs. Looking for anything amiss.

Nothing stands out at me. Sophie is a moody teenager. But aren't all teenagers moody? I know I certainly was. She'd rather get a ride home with her crush, rather than her father, but there's nothing surprising about that. Michael has always loved Sophie. From the minute she was born. *But has he loved her too much?*

He attends all of her basketball games, helps her with her studies, cares for her when she's sick. The same as he does for Hayley. I've never been able to tell the difference between his actual daughter and the one he has always treated like his own. It makes no sense. I track and kill predators for a living. Is it possible I could have missed one in my own home?

I'm not sure. But all I am left with is hours to mull it over. Nothingness that spans out in front of me for an eternity, until eventually, like the majority of women who are abducted, I die.

I refuse to die without knowing the truth, and so I decide that JC's attempt to unsettle me will also be the very thing that sets me free.

It may take a while to make it happen. Considering that I haven't eaten. Considering that the longer I am confined to this bed, the more my muscles will atrophy.

Last night, JC came in and stuck a needle in my vein and ran an IV line. After that he inserted a bladder catheter. He gives me a play by play, and although there's a fair amount of fight in me, I realize it is useless. This, and with all those fluids in me, it will be best not to have to lie in my own piss. He says he learned all of this on YouTube. Said it's amazing the kinds of things you can learn online. After I kicked him in the face, he wanted me to know that he's researching a technique that will sever my spinal cord, taking the use of my legs, but that will leave other sensations. Last thing he wants is to have to change my diapers for the rest of my life. And he'd like a baby. Before I get too old. He wants to see the pain of childbirth etched into my features and fall in love with me all over again.

That did it. One little comment can change your whole perspective. It made me realize what I had to do. Literally. I'd have to shit myself. If I made a real mess of it, he'd have to change me, and the linens too. He'd have to remove the restraints in order to clean me, and when it came right down to it, I realize that would not only be my best chance of escape, it will be my only chance.

WHEN I WAS YOUNG, AND THE NIGHT TERRORS CAME, MY MOTHER used to say that what happened in my dreams was far worse than anything that could happen in reality. How wrong she turned out to be about that. Wallowing in your own feces for ages is not all it's cracked up to be.

I was careful to wait until the room was dark. There are no windows in this room, but there is a skylight. Probably this is what saved me.

IN AND OUT. IN AND OUT. BREATHE. MY EYELIDS FLUTTER OPEN. I jolt upright, unsure if I'm dreaming or awake. I know something very bad has happened, but all the pieces are scattered in my mind, thousands of tiny fragments, my memory is hazy and incomplete, like a jigsaw puzzle, before you've worked out what it is supposed to be.

Thick liquid pools downward and wets my lashes, matting them together. Using the back of my hand, I brush the blood away. This is how I know I'm alive. There's so much blood.

But I'm alive. Injured, but alive.

He might be too.

I have to know. I can't stay here, in the perceived safety of this room. So long as he is breathing, safety doesn't exist. If he's not dead, this will never ever stop, and I really need it to end here. I make my way through the cabin, following the trail of blood—his or mine I'm not sure. The marble floor is heated under my feet, and the expanse of the cabin is surprising.

As I pass floor to ceiling windows, I stop at a grand fireplace, grabbing a fireplace poker. Gripping it tightly, I can't help but stare out at the view. It's mesmerizing. There's seemingly nothing but white for miles. Snow upon snow upon snow. No houses, no cars, no roads, no people. I scan the property. I see a small shed, and a long drive. A row of birdhouses suspended in the air. That's it. It's terrifyingly isolated. As remote as anything I've ever seen.

I hear something on the second floor. A creaking sound. I don't know the house well enough, or at all, to know if it's possible he could have made it up there.

Clutching the fire iron, I follow the trail of blood into the kitchen, knowing it will be the best place to find a weapon other than a fire iron. Although it will do, a knife would be better.

The kitchen is open, large, and it reminds me of a show kitchen, not one that has been lived in or well used. The blood specs have tapered off, and just beyond the massive island, I see him, slumped forward.

"Warren?" I say but my voice comes out tiny and foreign. It doesn't sound like me. It sounds like something is lodged in my throat. "JC, can you hear me?"

Silence. Other than a hiss or a creak from the deepest recesses of the house, here and there, it is eerily silent. Using the fire iron, I nudge him gently. His body falls to the right.

When he lands with an easy thud, I see the extent of the damage I have done. Slowly, it begins to come back to me. Him wiping my feces, a struggle ensuing. But then my mind goes blank. Shock, which acts as a protective mechanism, I know.

His face is torn off. Or rather *eaten* off. The bones that make up his nose, his eye sockets, and chin remain. But his flesh and some of the muscle is gone. His eyeballs bulge and flitter every once in a while, confirming that he is alive. His lips are missing, but his tongue is intact, or at least what is left of it. His teeth, once shiny and white, are now tinged with blood.

I've seen worse. Maybe. My stomach lurches forward, and I want to throw up, but relief takes over, pushing the bile down.

Now, I must focus.

I am in the middle of nowhere. I need to get out of here. I need to find a phone and a car, but first, clothes. My body is weak and bruised, and there is a severe gash at the base of my temple that I need to stop bleeding. My right hand is possibly broken. There is a dead man on the floor, his face half chewed off. The sun is sinking, the light will soon fade. But for now, I am safe.

Safe, as in to say, this bastard has me pretty good and well fucked. After striking him with the iron, just to ensure he's really done for, I reach down in search of a pulse. He flops forward, his eyes fixed on some faraway place. It's the first time, in all of my kills, that I've ever seen what it looks like under the skin on a person's face. Bile creeps its way up my throat. My stomach rolls.

I leave him, and then fumble through the cabinets, hoping to locate a first aid kit, some aspirin, and the knife drawer.

Walking over to where he is slumped, I flash the knife in front of his dead eyes. "Fancy a spinal cord severing?"

His body twitches, which gives me a good scare. The body is not always still, once it dies, and no matter how many times you've seen it happen, it's the sort of thing one never quite gets used to. If you've ever seen a skeleton without skin, you can imagine what he looks like. I have done an extensive amount of damage. There will be no open casket for him.

One minute I was laying in my own shit, my backside stinging, my own waste burning my skin. The next, he was changing me, unfastening my restraints, placing me in a tub of cold water.

I stared straight ahead, playing on the shock factor, while he sponged my body clean, while he lathered my hair with shampoo, while he shaved my legs, armpits, and pubic area. All the while, I stayed mute, silent, resigned.

Then when he was satisfied with his work, and he turned for the towel, I saw my opportunity and I took it. I lunged at him, knocking him off balance, my nails clawing at his skin, his eyeballs, my teeth tearing into his neck and face. I bit and chewed, and hit and clawed, until eventually his whole body went still. I tasted his blood and his flesh in my mouth, and my fingernails were full of bits and pieces of him.

I won, at least temporarily, but I did not come away unscathed. Sometime during our scuffle I had either been struck or had hit my head, and blood was raining down. It painted my naked body, and when I momentarily glanced in the mirror, I nearly smiled at the feral woman, staring back at me. I looked like a warrior painted in my own blood, mixed with the blood of my prey, unable to tell which was which.

And now in this kitchen, I look at him lying there. A pathetic excuse of a human. Now nothing more than a corpse.

I want nothing more than to get the fuck out of here, to find my way home. But I don't want to mess that situation up, either. While I have time to plot my next move, I plan to take it. And more than anything, I want to remember how I made him suffer.

MY ENTIRE BODY ACHES. IT ACHES WORSE THAN ANY PAIN I'VE EVER experienced, worse than the aftermath of childbirth, when your whole body feels like it has been hit by a Mack truck. Being tethered to a bed, being hung from the ceiling for hours, is, for me, new territory. I wonder what it will be like if I died here. Would anyone ever find me? Likely not. I only care because of the girls. It's hard to accept death when there's no body—believe me, I know.

I have to stop. I have to get it together. None of this matters now. I don't want to die. I am not going to die. *You have to move.* The whisper is urgent. Persistent. *You have to move, and you have to move now.*

I search the house, looking for a phone. Of course, I'm not that lucky. The only thing I find is a safe. No computer, no TV, no phone. Is that where he keeps it? Locked away? I know he has a cellphone. He said he'd been watching my house. Was it just another of his lies? I sink to the floor. I need to find keys, a car. I need to get out of this house. It would be stupid to walk out into the night in search of help. It's getting dark, I have no idea where I am, or even which direction to drive, even if I can manage to locate Warren's keys. This means I'm stuck here with his dead body until dawn unless by some miracle I manage to locate his cell. I pop two aspirin into my mouth and chase them down with a small amount of water. Ignoring the pain in my ankle, I stumble toward the bedroom and riffle through the drawers in search of clothes. It is not surprising to find that JC Warren is meticulous; everything is white and folded neatly, in identical fashion. I jostle through the clothing, looking for anything that might be hidden. In the end I find nothing, except for a pair of long johns, a baggy pair of men's jeans, a flannel, and wool socks that are too large for my feet. In the closet, I find a row of TVs, each screen showing a different area of the house. The display provides me with a good view of the rest of the house, and, creepily, the room I was in, with cameras mounted at multiple angles, Warren had a shot of me from all sides.

There is a shot into the garage where the old truck is, a vintage Bronco as it turns out. If I can't locate the keys, I may be able to hot wire it, an old trick my dad showed me once or twice, when my mother took his keys and refused to give them back. Those memories, situations that felt chaotic and awful at the time, now feel like a pot of gold at the end of a very shady rainbow.

When I scan the row of screens and locate the kitchen, my breath catches and hitches in my throat. Warren is not slumped over on the floor in the place that I left him.

Frantically, I scan the screens for movement. I see nothing. My knees grow weak and threaten to buckle.

Taking the fire iron from the dresser, I realize I have to make a decision. I have to take one or the other, but not both. The knife is too large, the blade too dangerous, to be stuffed into my pants.

I search the screens once more. There's no sign of him. Not in any of the shots. I consider that my mind could be playing tricks on me. Ultimately, I know better. Likely, there's a delay, and also, he would know how to avoid the cameras. I scan the images, going from room to room, trying to spot trails of blood. I'm just about to give up when I see it. In a bedroom down the hall, behind the door, a foot. He looks directly at the camera and flips the bird. Next thing I know, there are footsteps behind me. I can feel his breath on my neck. I catch a momentary glimpse of a handgun, almost as though he knew it would come to this. I swing at him, his fleshy barren face, lurching backward, his teeth bared. His eyeballs bulge, mere tissue in their sockets. They stare directly at me like an unspoken challenge.

CHAPTER THIRTY-ONE

Charlotte

I swing the fire iron as he fires the gun. I don't immediately realize that I have been hit—I am too busy swinging. I make contact with his head, landing a blow to his left temple. He goes down clutching the gun, but I do not give him a chance to aim or fire. Relentlessly, I strike him in the head again and again, until the walls are splattered with his blood and tufts of brain matter, reminiscent of the inside of a pumpkin, sticks to my arms and legs, and tiny bits of his skull are littered among the fibers of the carpet.

I don't stop for a long time, until there's almost nothing left of his head. My arms feel heavy and tired when I finally stop. They feel like jelly.

Nothing has ever felt more right than seeing his body there, his head obliterated. The nothingness in what's left of his eyes.

It's hard to know at first whose blood is whose, since I'm

covered in it from head to toe. Adrenaline floods my system, and for the first time in days, I feel no pain.

This, as it turns out, is not a good thing. The fire iron falls to the floor, and I begin to feel lightheaded. The room feels a little off kilter, and suddenly I start to panic, shedding myself of the bloody clothes. It's then that I see it: a small hole in my lower abdomen pumps out blood. I slink forward, bending over, clutching my waist. If I don't do something, I very well could bleed out right here on this floor, next to this corpse. This is not how I want to die, not after everything.

I stumble to the bathroom, clutching my side, walking like the hunchback of Notre Dame. I search under the cabinets for a first aid kit, something with which to stop the bleeding, but find nothing save for a couple of towels and a roll of toilet paper.

Back to the bedroom I go, where I grab a shirt from his dresser and fold it, pressing it to the wound. All of a sudden, I am very cold, ceaselessly shivering, but also naked. In any case, it isn't good.

Using a T-shirt and a roll of duct tape, I fix a makeshift bandage. I throw on another set of clothes and rummage through the kitchen, ultimately grabbing a handful of bottles of water, a loaf of bread, and a bunch of bananas.

The bananas are the last thing I remember before my whole world goes black.

CHAPTER THIRTY-TWO

Charlotte

When I come to, I am sprawled out on the marble floor. My head aches, and my vision is blurry. I'm certain I have suffered a concussion as a result of passing out and hitting the floor.

Terribly slowly, I pull myself over to a chair and slothfully manage to get myself to a seated position. From there, after several failed and painful attempts, I manage to stand.

It takes me an eternity, but eventually I stumble from the kitchen out to the garage, where I attempt to hot wire the Bronco. It takes the better part of two hours before I am forced to give up. I am too tired and too cold to go on.

If I'm going to die, there are worse places I can think of to do it.

Still, I know better than to fall asleep. I can't be sure it won't be a permanent situation. Fumbling through the sack of items from the kitchen, I open the loaf of bread and remove a slice, tearing the tiniest pieces, slipping them onto my tongue. I am not particularly hungry, but I'll do whatever it takes to keep me from losing consciousness. I need all of the energy and strength I can get. It's then that I think of the IV back in the bedroom. If Warren had those supplies, he is bound to have others. Unfortunately, it's too late to go back. I know I cannot summon the strength it would take to stumble back to the house and up those stairs. I would die trying. And I refuse to die in that house.

I HEAR A MOTOR RUNNING, AND I THINK I MUST BE DREAMING. When I open my eyes, beacons of light filter in through the garage door. When I look down, I can see that I have bled through the T-shirt.

"Hello?" I hear a voice call. "Warren?"

There's a knocking sound, followed by a car door opening and shutting. I don't have the energy to make it to the garage door opener attached to the wall on time. I hear the truck shift into reverse. I let my eyes close and drift off toward darkness. Suddenly, I am sitting in my father's pickup truck in front of the county feed store. "I'll just be a minute, peanut," he says to me. "If anyone tries to get in, you just lay on the horn."

My eyes shoot open, and I give everything left in me to pressing down on that horn.

MY EYELIDS ARE HEAVY, BUT I FORCE THEM OPEN. IT TAKES SEVERAL tries before I'm able to get a grip on what I'm seeing. Everything is a blur. My fist is tightly wrapped around a white sheet. I flex my toes. Overhead, bright lights whiz by. A woman leans down. She has the face of an angel. "You're going into surgery. You're going to be just fine."

She can't obviously know that I am going to be just fine, I think. But I like it that she lies. How terrible it would be for anything else to be the final words I hear.

I don't know if I will be fine. But at this point, I have nothing left in me with which to care.

I drift off and dream of my dad. I think of what he said to me the day I came home from my waitressing shift to find a crib up in the spare bedroom. I told him I didn't intend to live in his house forever. That I was sorry. I had never meant to add more to his plate. I told him I knew I'd messed up. He looked me straight in the eye and he said, "It's not about the falling down, Charlotte. It's about the staying down. And I know you. You won't stay down for long. "

I WAKE UP IN RECOVERY. I DON'T FEEL PAIN. I DON'T FEEL anything. "It went well," a steady voice says. I can't see the face that belongs to the voice that speaks to me, but I can smell her perfume. Something delicate. She stands at the head of my bed, pressing buttons on a monitor. "We were able to stop the bleeding."

She doesn't offer any further information, and I don't ask. I watch as she moves purposefully around the room, checking and rechecking her work. Eventually she pushes something through my IV line, and before I know it, I once again drift off into oblivion.

The next time I open my eyes, there are police officers standing at my bedside. I close my eyes and pretend to be too tired and too traumatized to talk. I'm heavily drugged, and I'm afraid of what I might say.

MICHAEL STANDS NEXT TO ME. SO DOES THE FBI. MY HUSBAND'S face looks serious, if not sympathetic. On instinct I start to cry. He places his hand on mine. It's large and cold and very familiar. Full, chest-heaving, snot-bubbling sobs spill out of me. Eventually, the men offer to leave and give us privacy, and the nurse asks if I'd like something to help calm me. "You don't have to tell them anything you don't want to, Charlotte," Michael says when we're finally alone. "You know that."

He's right. I do know that.

I'm aware that I cannot tell them everything. But I can tell them a lot.

"I'm sorry," he tells me, spooning ice chips into my mouth. He doesn't elaborate on what he's apologizing for, and I do my best to look like I don't know.

"You have nothing to be sorry for," I reply, surprised at how easily the lie slips off my tongue. "You told me I needed to cut back on work. I should have listened. Now—"

"This isn't your fault." He places the cup of ice on the table and smooths the matted hair away from my face. His lies, too, flow effortlessly. His expression, his demeanor, is the same as it ever was. As long as we've lived together, as long as I've known him, nearly two decades now, I thought I could tell when he was being dishonest. But here in this hospital bed, in God knows where, I can see that this isn't true.

My life hangs precariously in his hands. I know. I watched JC Warren's footage. Which is why I do my best to pretend.

He leans down and kisses my face. "We don't have to do that thing where we pretend anymore, darling."

"What do you mean?"

"I know you've been through a lot."

I look away toward the window. It's dark out.

"I'm just so glad you got out of that house."

I think of the cabin. Of the abundance of evidence contained inside. Who knew what JC Warren had hidden there? He knew an awful lot about my life. Or at least he pretended to.

As though he is reading my thoughts, Michael walks over to the door, and then back toward the bed. "They thought you were inside. They thought you were gone. I thought I lost you."

"I was inside."

Michael cocks his head. "Do you remember anything about what happened before you were found?"

I feign ignorance. "Not really."

"The fire, Charlotte. It was bad."

"The fire."

His face remains neutral. "The girls have been so worried. They wanted to come, but I took the first flight out. I didn't know what condition I'd find you in. They wouldn't tell me anything."

"And now? Are they okay? Do they know I'm fine?"

"They're with my mom."

"Good," I say. "I think they should stay there."

"For a bit, yes. I agree." That's what he says. But it's what he doesn't say that really counts. He doesn't say that I've been nothing more than a tool for him, all these years, all this time. He doesn't say that he sought me out, that he's been lying to me all along. He doesn't say that his architecture firm is a front, that he's been heading the agency all along.

He doesn't tell me any of the things I heard watching and listening to JC Warren's recordings from inside our home. He simply says, "The press is all over this. As you can imagine."

He doesn't know what I know. He doesn't know *if* I know anything at all. So, he doesn't explain why he's used me to take out his competition—he doesn't say it's because he is the biggest pedophile of all.

I don't say it either.

There's time for that.

CHAPTER THIRTY-THREE

Charlotte

Michael was right. The media is all over this. It is apparently a story worth chasing. All the way to Alaska, and of course, they are geared up and waiting back home. The cost of fame, violence against women—whether or not my profession, flight attending as a whole, is sexist. It's all laid out there, to be pored over, discussed ceaselessly, my life examined under a microscope.

This does not make for a good situation. My husband doesn't say it but I can tell. He wishes I'd died in that fire. Most likely that was his intention when he had it set. He hadn't known, couldn't have known— that I was in the garage—that a kind neighbor seeing the log cabin go up in flames would rush over to make sure everyone got out okay.

After my surgery, I am not allowed to travel for several weeks.

After five days, Michael returns to Texas.

Although they will remain in his mother's care, he wants to

check on the girls. I have FaceTimed them every day. They are eager for me to get home. But I am certain they are nowhere near as eager as I am.

THREE WEEKS AFTER I WAS RESCUED, I AM FINALLY ABLE TO RETURN home to my own bed. Despite the physical therapy and sheer determination, I am still fairly reliant on Michael to do most things for me.

The press once again has rained down on us, on our street, on our neighborhood. I even supposedly have best friends I've never even met. Everyone talks like they have something new to say, something that has never been said before. A group of "Justice Warriors" were detained last week, and from what I learn online, most groups have started to fizzle out. Hard crime is a bit much for your average homemaker, I suppose. It isn't all a disappointment. It's not all a waste. There are well-wishers, flowers, cards, meals, and an overflowing Fund Me account.

Michael excels at playing the concerned and caring husband, and I am more than happy to let him.

So long as we have all of this attention on us, it will be difficult for him to do anything drastic where I am concerned. The girls are safe and moderately happy at his mother's, and this buys me time to come up with a plan.

"I don't know if you should return to work, you know, after..." he says one morning over coffee. "We have enough money in the Fund Me account...I was thinking you could take some time and...I don't know...relax. Or maybe write that book you've always talked about."

The sentiment makes me smile. "We'll see."

It's funny how different he looks now that I don't care about him anymore. Now, I can see how ordinary he is, how it was my love that made him special, that made it seem like he was a good husband and father—that placed him on a pedestal.

But in all honesty, it was more than love that made me fall for Michael. Our relationship started out as transactional in nature, and it will end that way too.

My father used to say that about police work. The way things end are often the way they start. I never really gave much thought to what he meant, but it makes sense.

Earlier this week, I had a long conversation with Hayley over FaceTime. She is having problems with the same boy I nearly dosed with laxatives. *If only.* "There is a fundamental truth I have learned," I said to her. "If you aren't certain of who you are and what you want, you will attract people all too eager to guide you into finding those answers."

"Speak English," she huffed.

"I am. Hayley, there are endless people," I told her. "People with endless opinions, rules, requirements, and suggestions for how you should live your life, for how you should behave, but none of them are able to take into consideration the only thing that matters: they cannot truly understand, nor do they care about your desires in the way you do, so they are not in any way equipped to guide you."

"Elliot isn't trying to *guide* me, mom. He's trying to date me."

"No, Hayley. He's trying to manipulate you."

"You don't know that."

"Then why are we having this conversation?"

"Because you asked."

"Look," I said. "Even when people have the very best of intentions, and even *if* they're attempting to be unselfish, it is never possible for them to separate their desire for you from their own desire for themselves. That's why—if you listen—if you give in— if you allow yourself to be led, without asking *what* it is they want from you, or who and what it is they want you to be, you will always be playing a losing game."

One night, the same week as that conversation with Hayley, I am in bed when Michael gets in. Although I'm not yet fully asleep, I'm not in the mood for playing nice, for make-believe, and so I pretend. I listen as he climbs into bed. It makes my skin crawl to have to sleep next to a man who would harm my child, but life is full of hard things.

He rolls over and kisses my cheek, and whispers, "Tell me, Charlotte. What are you supposed to do when you can't let something go, but you can't kill it either?" And just for a moment, I can't be sure I'm not dreaming.

I AM HOME FOR SIX DAYS WHEN MICHAEL'S MOM BRINGS THE GIRLS home. I have learned a lot in that time. A thorough search of my husband's computer tells me many things that I need to know, but not everything. I will need to talk with Sophie about her father. And it will need to happen soon. I refuse to let him near my children, but prison time, while perhaps the simplest solution, does not feel like enough. Furthermore, it will further thrust my family into the spotlight; having to give a deposition, and possibly testify, will only further damage my daughter. She has already suffered enough. She does not need to lose her anonymity, too.

Plus, I could never live with myself, knowing I've killed other men for less. Rotting in a prison cell is not enough.

A scan of Michael's computer tells me that JC Warren was right about most of what he said. Michael is trading and selling girls and has been for some time. While he doesn't do the heavy lifting, so to speak, encrypted emails prove that he is definitely involved. He is the mastermind.

He has a lot of money in offshore accounts, some of which he hides in real estate. Under various aliases. But there's more. Michael has other children. Multiple children with multiple women, most of them born to young women who are either incarcerated for prostitution, drugs, or who are missing or dead. Four daughters and a son, all younger than Hayley. It is unclear where they reside. But he provides for them monetarily.

HOW IS IT POSSIBLE TO LIVE WITH A STRANGER, WHEN ALL ALONG you thought it was you who had all the secrets? A question I have asked myself endlessly. Maybe that was a part of the scam. It's hard to see truth about others when you're so busy trying to conceal it yourself. When I look in the mirror, I look like a shell of who I used to be. My life today compared to six weeks ago is nearly unrecognizable.

Suffice it to say, my self-esteem is not at an all-time high.

I do not consider myself to be a stupid person, and yet, I have managed to ignore the reality of my situation for years. Meanwhile, seemingly everyone around me saw through Michael and his lies. Even my own daughter.

Was I meant to be one of his girls, back at the very beginning when he showed up at that fraternity party? Is that why he was there? He was obviously older—was he in search of prey? Had he planned this from the very beginning? Realizing that the answer is likely yes makes me physically sick. And yet, it changes nothing.

AFTER I AM CERTAIN MICHAEL IS ASLEEP, I SNEAK INTO SOPHIE'S room, where I shake her awake. "Soph—"

Her eyes shoot open, and I wonder how many times she's done this before. How many times has she been terrified? And worse?

"Sophie," I say through gritted teeth, perching myself on the edge of her bed. "I need to ask you something, and I need you to be honest with me."

Her face falls, but she recovers quickly. "Is it about the money?"

"The money? No."

"Oh," she says. "Because I told him you'd find out. I mean...I knew you would."

I feel like I'm going to throw up. Not only has he been molesting my daughter, he's been paying for her silence. "'Sophie," I say wincing. "Soph—I'm so sorry. I know I haven't been around a lot."

"That's not true," she tells me, sensing trouble. "You're around."

"Sophie, I need to know..." I pause and scan the room. Chewing at my bottom lip, I say, "I need to know if your father has been hurting you."

Her brow furrows. "Hurting me?"

"Yes. Hurting you. Has he behaved in any way inappropriately with you...sexually?"

She scoots backward on the bed. "Ew. No. Why would you say such a thing?" Her face twists and finally she cocks her head as though she's just remembered something. "Wait. Are you on drugs?"

"No. I'm serious, Sophie. This is not something you should lie to me about."

She scoots to the edge of the bed and stands up. "I can't believe you! I can't believe you'd ask me that! Dad would never hurt me. You know that."

Suddenly, all of that pent up teenage anger shows itself and she bares her teeth. Suddenly, I'm inclined to believe her. Suddenly, I realize the rage she is exhibiting is not entirely genuine. She is hiding something. "The money...what were you talking about?"

"Nothing," she scoffs. "Get out."

"Sophie. You're going to tell me the truth. And you're going to tell me now."

"It's not that big of a deal. Dad was right. You're going to make it this huge thing. You act like I'm a child!"

"Dad was right about what?"

"That you'd say he should be saving his money. That I should want to pitch in for free."

My eyes close. I can't bring myself to open them. "Pitch in how?"

"With the lists."

"What lists?"

"The lists of girls on social media."

"Soph—I need you to spell it out for me. What are you doing with lists on social?"

"I make friends with the girls. Then Dad goes after their family for business."

"Business? What business?"

She looks at me like I've grown three heads. "For his architecture stuff. It's all about seven degrees of separation, you know. Marketing...life..."

"Oh, Sophie." I can't bring myself to tell her the truth. Her father has been paying her blood money to do really bad things.

CHAPTER THIRTY-FOUR

Charlotte

When we land in Cabo, a local man, who is not old, but not young, offers to show us around. He offers to carry our bags, recommend restaurants, and the best sightseeing tours. "I can take you to the whales," he says in a strident voice.

Michael says all he wants is to get to the hotel. I'm really glad I didn't rush this. "Maybe," I suggest, eyeing the girls. "Whale watching could be fun."

The man's eyes shine. "Where is your hotel? I can take you."

"We have a car lined up," Michael tells him.

The man, weathered by the sun, studies him, a serious expression on his face.

It's the first time I feel like I can truly breathe in weeks. Inhaling deeply, the man smells like salt, fish, and freedom. I feel a sense of calm rush over me. Luckily, convincing Michael to take a family trip over spring break turned out to be easier than I'd expected. He agreed that we could use some time away as a family. Some time to allow the dust to settle a bit.

"You should be careful," he says to Michael as he looks at me. "The cartels. Hard to know who to trust."

With a nod and a clipped tone, Michael assures the man we'll be fine.

As we step out into the day, it's sunny and beautiful, and the girls seem happy. I do not let them out of my sight. I know how easy it is to disappear here.

The sun and the sand and the carefree feeling of having no particular place you need to be makes me wish we'd taken more trips like this. Before. Back when things were different, back when I hadn't known the truth. I've been thinking about that a lot as I've recovered—this is one of the things about being out of commission, the endless, uninterrupted hours in which to think. What a gift it is, to be naive. To live your life believing it is one way, absent of the truth.

Last week Michael and I were discussing a project he is working on and he said to me, "If you knew something was going to end badly, but that it was going to be really beautiful along the way...would you still do it?"

I cocked my brow. "How beautiful are we talking?"

"One of the most beautiful experiences in your life kind of beautiful."

The answer came easily. "Then, yes," I said. "Yes, I would."

IF I'D RUSHED THIS TRIP, I NEVER WOULD HAVE BEEN ABLE TO gather the information I needed. For weeks, I have worked hard at pretending all is normal. Or as close to normal as normal can get, considering. Thinking of Henry, I kept the six Ps in mind: Prior planning prevents piss poor performance. That notion, he always said, is at the forefront of every good job.

Speaking of jobs, there was so much I wanted to find out before I could get rid of the one person who held all of the answers. The lists of accounts, being one. It turns out, Michael was smart enough to open payable-on-death accounts with me listed as the beneficiary. With the exception of an accountant, he simply forgot to mention they existed.

But there were other things too. Things more important than money. The list of names. Buyers and sellers, traders and abductors. A treasure trove of data. Very bad people who deserve to pay. Then there are the missing girls, and the places where they might be found. That is, if they're still alive.

IT'S STRANGE WATCHING YOUR HUSBAND AND CHILDREN, HAVING their last best day. It's not as easy as you might think, when you're the only one who knows what's coming. I wanted to make it special, for all of them. I thought back on my last, best day. Before I knew the truth about Michael.

Before I realized my life amounted to a bigger lie than I'd thought.

Back when the biggest annoyances of my life were carpool, making lunches, and scheduled sex.

Watching the three of them on the boat, lounging on the deck, laughing at something Hayley has said, Michael looks up, his face scanning the boat. He's looking for me. He's thinking I shouldn't be missing this, and it's genuine. Or at least it seems that way. I smile, hold up one finger, and finish mixing our drinks.

"This was a great idea," he tells me when I finally make my way over, and I'm glad for the man at the airport. I'm glad I took his advice. I'm glad I chartered this boat in hopes that we might see whales.

The sky is cloudless, and the day feels like the ocean, like it might go on forever. The girls are as happy as I've seen them in recent weeks. The permanent look of worry, or dread, or both, has nearly vanished. Their eyes are once again bright. It pains me to know this is all temporary, that all of life is. That we can only hold on to these moments in our mind.

I take a lot of photos. No one complains like they usually would.

My favorite is one of Michael standing on the edge of the boat, looking into the ocean, one hand clasped in Sophie's, the other in Hayley's. At the last second, he looks over his shoulder at the camera, at me as if to say, can you believe this?

He smiles, and then he jumps.

MICHAEL WAS TRAVELING IN A TEN-PASSENGER VAN WITH A GROUP from our hotel, on their way to a golf course seven miles south, when they were ambushed by the cartel. He was shot seventeen times. Only two of the ten passengers survived. Michael was not one of them.

Maybe it was a case of mistaken identity. But only two people will probably ever know for sure. Me and the weathered man from the airport.

The girls and I are lounging when the police find us at the hotel pool.

They escort us to a small office just off the lobby of the hotel. There are only two chairs. A third is brought in, but I have already pulled Hayley onto my lap. On the desk is a porcelain dolphin, on the wall, an aerial shot of the hotel. It looks dated, and I wonder how much has changed in the time since it was taken.

Two police officers enter the room, different than the ones who escorted us in the first place. Water pools on the floor at my feet. Towels are offered, and from there everything else happens fast.

They ask me to confirm my identity, for identification, but I explain that it is all in the room. They ask where Michael is, and when I confirm he is golfing, they deliver the news.

Even though I know what they are going to say, it hits me harder than I expect. All the years we spent together flash before my eyes, snapshots of love and lies. But more than any of that, the countless memories I can cast aside, it is the girls' wailing that threatens to do me in.

HOW UNLUCKY CAN ONE FAMILY BE? THAT IS WHAT EVERYONE IS thinking when the news hits. Even if it isn't what they're saying, it's what they're thinking.

On the flight home, later that same afternoon, I am thinking about the other families making the same trip, returning home, with broken hearts, to empty houses. I could ask whether or not I did the right thing, although I know that to do so would be pointless.

Lives were lost. But countless others will be saved.

It's about balance, I suppose.

There is a lot of work ahead. It makes me think of my mother, of how easy it would have been just to get up and walk away. How easy it still could be.

For now, I am here. The girls are not yet ready to know the truth about their father. It's not an easy concept to grasp that something can be both good and bad, and sometimes it's better to lose a thing slowly, rather than all at once.

The time will come, eventually, where I will have to sit them down and explain everything. It is inevitable. Otherwise things cannot go according to plan.

EPILOGUE

Charlotte

Nine months later

I stop at a cafe and use the bathroom to change and do my makeup. Shaking out the short blonde wig, folded neatly into my oversized Hermes handbag, I slip it into place. Then, I touch up my lipstick, check my reflection, add another coat of mascara, and still unsatisfied, I make the effort to slip the false eyelashes into place. I close my eyes and squeeze them shut, before opening them slowly, carefully checking my appearance one last time. The transformation makes me smile. I look nothing like myself.

When Sophie comes out of the stall, her eyes widen in surprise. Mine too. Her brown eyes painted black, in combination with the red lipstick and super short skirt, terrify me. She doesn't look like my daughter. She looks like me.

"Should we go over it again?" I ask, glancing at her in the mirror.

"No," she says. "I told you a thousand times. I got it."

WE MEET NUMBER TWO ON THE LIST, IAN MILLER, AT HIS PARENT'S fortieth anniversary party. We are, of course, not on the guest list, but like most things, this, too, can easily be fixed. I concoct a plausible story. If asked, I will say my company does business with the Millers' company. Not wanting to seem oblivious, or embarrass themselves, the Millers are too highbrow to press for more.

Sophie and I make ourselves at home. Together we get acquainted with the layout of the estate and the who's who of the guest list. When the time comes, we toast the older Millers.

At dinner, during the third course, Ian Miller excuses himself to take a call. To the rich, work never ceases. But the call is probably more pleasure than work, which is why it gives me great satisfaction to interrupt it.

Eventually, we meet in the bathroom. It's horrific, black with flecks of gold thrown in. Sometimes the rich have taste. More often than not, they don't. Closing the door quietly behind me, I press my back against it, and taking a deep breath, I fish my gloves from my small clutch.

Ian Miller finishes his piss and only then does he turn around.

"I have heard about you," he says to me. "Charlotte, right?"

Our eyes meet. He is charming, this one. Maybe in a different life, I would have locked the door and turned the water on full blast for other reasons. It's a pity, really.

"The female assassin."

"What a funny way to put it. An assassin is just an assassin, no?"

"I suppose you haven't come to make small talk—or pose philosophical questions."

"I suppose not."

"Well then, you'd better get on with it." His tone is neutral but his eyes are sad. I estimate he has a bit of fight in him.

"Do you want to die?"

"Few people want to die, my dear Charlotte."

It is a power play to call me by my real name and not Olivia, like everyone else. "I am not your dear."

"You are the last face I will see alive, so that makes you special, no?"

"No."

He takes a step forward. "How do you want to do this? Shall I sit? Kneel? Stand, like so? In other words, how do you want me?"

"As you are is fine."

"Okay," he says, holding his arms up in surrender. "I am ready."

I am angry that he is making this so effortless. It is not fair, not after I've come so far, all the way to Switzerland, that he is removing all of the satisfaction. He knows exactly what he is doing.

Taking a step forward, I open my switchblade.

"To answer your question," he stutters, "I am not ready to die and leave all of this. Who would be?"

"But you aren't going to fight?"

"A woman, no. Never."

I don't believe him. "Then, although it will be a lie, I will say in advance that I am sorry. I didn't take you for stupid."

"It doesn't make sense, I know. I suppose not to someone like you."

I check my watch. "I'm terribly sorry, but you're right. I don't have time for small talk. It's almost time to cut the cake. Chocolate mousse, I hear. My favorite."

"At some point," he says, "you just stop running."

"Tell me about it," I say. He swings at me and I duck. I lift the knife above my head and stab him in the eye. For all the girls. For all the videos. Because I can.

He swings again, but his reflexes are not fast enough, thanks to the additive that Sophie slipped in his drink. "You're evil," he chokes out as I twist the blade.

"You're right," I say, and then I slide the knife out and slit his throat.

"An eye for an eye," the weathered man tells me with a chuckle. "Leave it to you to take it to a whole new level."

"Go fuck yourself." He isn't supposed to be in Switzerland, but he's of the overbearing and protective variety, and it's safe to say we haven't gotten that part sorted out yet.

"Careful, dear. You'll bleed on people who didn't cut you."

My stomach clinches. Henry used to say that.

In a way, Carlo is my new Henry, although Henry he could never be. It was him who had arranged for the hit on Michael. He didn't have to meet me at the airport, but he did, which meant that I liked him right away, in that love-hate kind of way you do with a handler. Regardless, he is everything I need in my life right now.

"Basel is beautiful, yes?" he says to Sophie.

She kind of shrugs, and he looks at me. "Teenagers."

"She's just mad I wouldn't let her keep the clothes."

Carlo smiles. "Your mother is right. The clothes you cannot keep. They go with the job."

Sophie stares at her fingernails, picking at a piece of chipped polish. "There will be more where that came from. Don't worry."

She looks up at me expectantly. "Can we go shopping now?"

"Basel is not the place for shopping," Carlo says. "Wait until you get to Zurich."

"Can I go look around?" she asks, pointing toward the door.

"No," I say firmly. "In a minute, we will go."

My phone chimes, and I check my messages. It's a reminder

from my assistant that it's time to wire the monthly payment for Michael's other children to their Nona, the lady who cares for them. I haven't met them, and I don't know that I will. Although, who knows? Maybe someday. "Mom?" Sophie whines. "Can I? Please."

Carlo gives me the once-over. "She will be fine. Basel is safe. You have trained her well. I say let her go."

"She is not ready yet."

"You are the one who is not ready."

"Yes," I say. "I am the one who is not ready."

"This is a problem, Olivia. If you hold on too tight."

"It is equally a problem if you let go too soon."

There is a roar of laughter in the corner of the cafe. "Your favor has been repaid," Carlo remarks. "Ian Miller is dead. I can sleep at night."

"That's the problem with favors," I say to him, every bit for Sophie's benefit. "Eventually, you have to pay them back."

"He killed my daughter," he says to Sophie, who is both unaware and unconcerned by the fact that we seem to be talking circles around her. "She was younger than you are now."

Snow has begun to fall in the street. I stare out at it for a long time and think of Michael. "You won't sleep," I say to Carlo.

He looks at me knowingly. "You are right. It is never enough."

"So this list," Sophie mentions. "The one my mother is always talking about...you've seen it?"

"The kill list."

Sophie shrugs. "Sure."

"No," he says, glancing at me. "I'm afraid that is all your mother."

AT THE COUNTER OF A CAFE ON RUE DU MARCHÉ IN ZURICH, I stand in line, waiting to place an order for two coffees and a pastry for Sophie. The line is long, and the doors to the shop open so frequently that the cold air from the street continuously spills in. The line snakes itself around a giant fireplace, which I use to warm my hands.

Outside, it has begun to drizzle. It comes down in waves, the kind of steady downfall you know is bound to turn into heavy rain. Later it will snow. I text Hayley back home. She has a dance recital tomorrow, and Michael's mother is helping her get ready. I tell her I am sad to miss it. She promises to send a video.

"It's nice, isn't it?" the voice in front of me says. I don't realize at first that he is speaking to me until he repeats a version of the question, and I recognize the accent as decidedly American. "It's not usually this busy," he says. "Must be the rain. And the holidays."

I respond with a tight smile.

"You're American, also, no?"

Another smile.

"You can always tell."

"Is that right?"

"Maybe just wishful thinking…makes it feel a little less lonely. Being so far from home."

"Home is where you make it, I think."

He seems surprised for a moment, but he doesn't say anything, and he doesn't let on why.

"I'm John," he says, extending his hand.

I know who you are. I smile and place my hand in his. *You're number four on the list.* "Olivia."

Later in his apartment, he builds a fire, and we lay naked, curled in front of it. The flames are warm and inviting, but also dangerous. He nuzzles my ear, and I think of the knife in my purse. The coolness of the blade, the firmness of its handle. It reminds me of him, in a way. Smooth and necessary.

"Can you stay?"

Staring at the fire, I think about his question, about what he is really asking. He is handsome, and a gentleman, and the best lay I've had in a very long time. He could be useful, so I say, "For a little while."

"Do you have a fireplace back home, Olivia?"

"No," I tell him. "And I've missed it my whole life."

A NOTE FROM BRITNEY

Dear Reader,

I hope you enjoyed reading *Kill, Sleep, Repeat.*

Writing a book is an interesting adventure, it's a bit like inviting people into your brain to rummage around. *Look where my imagination took me. These are the kind of stories I like...*

That feeling is often intense and unforgettable. And mostly, a ton of fun.

With that in mind—thank you again for reading my work. I don't have the backing or the advertising dollars of big publishing, but hopefully I have something better... readers who like the same kind of stories I do. If you are one of them, please share with your friends and consider helping out by doing one (or all) of these quick things:

1. Visit my review page and write a 30 second review (even short ones make a big difference).

(http://britneyking.com/aint-too-proud-to-beg-for-reviews/)

Many readers don't realize what a difference reviews make but they make ALL the difference.

2. Drop me an email and let me know you left a review. This way I can enter you into my monthly drawing for signed paperback copies.

(hello@britneyking.com)

3. Point your psychological thriller loving friends to their free copies of my work. My favorite friends are those who introduce me to books I might like. **(http://www.britneyking.com)**

4. If you'd like to make sure you don't miss anything, to receive an email whenever I release a new title, sign up for my new release newsletter.

(https://britneyking.com/new-release-alerts/)

Thanks for helping, and for reading my work. It means a lot.

Britney King

Austin, Texas

June 2019

ABOUT THE AUTHOR

Britney King lives in Austin, Texas with her husband, children, a dog named Gatsby, one ridiculous cat, and a partridge in a peach tree.

When she's not wrangling the things mentioned above, she writes psychological, domestic and romantic thrillers set in suburbia.

Without a doubt, she thinks connecting with readers is the best part of this gig. You can find Britney online here:

Email: britney@britneyking.com
Web: https://britneyking.com
Facebook: https://www.facebook.com/BritneyKingAuthor
Instagram: https://www.instagram.com/britneyking_/
Twitter: https://twitter.com/BritneyKing_
Goodreads: https://bit.ly/BritneyKingGoodreads
Pinterest: https://www.pinterest.com/britneyking_/

Happy reading.

ACKNOWLEDGMENTS

Many thanks to my family and friends for the endless inspiration and for your support in my creative endeavors.

To the beta team, ARC team, and the bloggers. You make this gig a blast.

Last, but certainly not least, I'd like to thank you for reading this. If not for you, I'd have to get what a couple of family members (who shall remain nameless) like to call a "real job." :)

Thank you for making this dream of mine come true.

I appreciate you.

ALSO BY BRITNEY KING

Room 553

Room 553 is a standalone psychological thriller. Vivid and sensual, Room 553 weaves a story of cruelty, reckless lust, and blind, bloody justice.

HER

HER is a standalone psychological thriller which covers the dark side of female relationships. But equally—it's about every relationship anyone has ever had they knew was terrible for them. It's for those of us who swam for the deep end anyway, treading water because it seemed like more fun than sitting on the sidelines. It's about the lessons learned along the way. And knowing better the next time. Or not.

The Social Affair | Book One

The Replacement Wife | Book Two

Speak of the Devil | Book Three

The New Hope Series Box Set

The New Hope Series offers gripping, twisted, furiously clever reads that demand your attention, and keep you guessing until the very end. For fans of the anti-heroine and stories told in unorthodox ways, *The New Hope Series* delivers us the perfect dark and provocative villain. The only question—who is it?

Water Under The Bridge | Book One

Dead In The Water | Book Two

Come Hell or High Water | Book Three

The Water Series Box Set

The Water Trilogy follows the shady love story of unconventional married couple—he's an assassin—she kills for fun. It has been compared to a crazier book version of Mr. and Mrs. Smith. Also, Dexter.

Bedrock | Book One

Breaking Bedrock | Book Two

Beyond Bedrock | Book Three

The Bedrock Series Box Set

The Bedrock Series features an unlikely heroine who should have known better. Turns out, she didn't. Thus she finds herself tangled in a messy, dangerous, forbidden love story and face-to-face with a madman hell-bent on revenge. The series has been compared to Fatal Attraction, Single White Female, and Basic Instinct.

Around The Bend

Around The Bend, is a heart-pounding standalone which traces the journey of a well-to-do suburban housewife, and her life as it unravels, thanks to the secrets she keeps. If she were the only one with things she wanted to keep hidden, then maybe it wouldn't have turned out so bad. But she wasn't.

Somewhere With You | Book One

Anywhere With You | Book Two

The With You Series Box Set

The With You Series at its core is a deep love story about unlikely friends who travel the world; trying to find themselves, together and apart. Packed with drama and adventure along with a heavy dose of suspense, it has been compared to The Secret Life of Walter Mitty and Love, Rosie.

SNEAK PEEK: THE SOCIAL AFFAIR

BOOK ONE

In the tradition of *Gone Girl* and *Behind Closed Doors* comes a gripping, twisted, furiously clever read that demands your attention, and keeps you guessing until the very end. For fans of the anti-heroine and stories told in unorthodox ways, *The Social Affair* delivers us the perfect dark and provocative villain. The only question—who is it?

A timeless, perfect couple waltzes into the small coffee shop where Izzy Lewis works. Instantly enamored, she does what she always does in situations like these: she searches them out on social media.

Just like that—with the tap of a screen— she's given a front row seat to the Dunns' picturesque life. This time, she's certain she's found what she's been searching for. This time, she'll go to whatever lengths it takes to ensure she gets it right—even if this means doing the unthinkable.

Intense and original, The Social Affair is a disturbing psychological thriller that explores what can happen when privacy is traded for convenience.

What readers are saying:

"Another amazingly well-written novel by Britney King. It's every bit as dark, twisted and mind twisting as Water Under The Bridge...maybe even a little more so."

"Hands down- best book by Britney King. Yet. She has delivered a difficult writing style so perfectly and effortlessly, that you just want to worship the book for the writing. The author has managed to make murder/assassination/accidental- gunshot- to-the-head-look easy. Necessary."

"Having fallen completely head over heels for these characters and this author with the first book in the series, I've been pretty much salivating over the thought of this book for months now. You'll be glad to know that it did not disappoint!"

Praise

"If Tarantino were a woman and wrote novels... they might read a bit like this."

"Fans of Gillian Flynn and Paula Hawkins meet your next obsession."

"Provocative and scary."

"A dark and edgy page-turner. What every good thriller is made of."

"I devoured this novel in a single sitting, absolutely enthralled by the storyline. The suspense was clever and unrelenting!"

"Completely original and complex."

"Compulsive and fun."

"No-holds-barred villains. Fine storytelling full of mystery and suspense."

"Fresh and breathtaking insight into the darkest corners of the human psyche."

THE SOCIAL AFFAIR

BRITNEY KING

COPYRIGHT

To those who've walked into our lives without first asking permission...

PROLOGUE

Attachment is an awfully hard thing to break. I should know. I surface from the depths of sleep to complete and utter darkness. I don't want to open my eyes. I have to. "I warned you, and I warned you," I hear his voice say. It's not the first time. He called out to me, speaking from the edge of consciousness, back when I thought this all might have been a dream. It's too late for wishful thinking now. This is his angry voice, the one I best try to avoid. My mind places it immediately. This one is reserved for special occasions, the worst of times.

I hear water running in the background. Or at least I think I do. For my sake, I hope I'm wrong. I try to recall what I was doing before, but this isn't that kind of sleep. It's the heavy kind, the kind you wake from and hardly know what year you're in, much less anything else. I consider how much time might have passed since I dozed off. Then it hits me.

"You really shouldn't have done that," he says, and his eyes come into focus. Those eyes, there's so much history in them; it's all still there now. I see it reflected back to me. I read a quote once that said... a true mark of maturity is when someone hurts you, and you try to understand their situation instead of trying to hurt them back. This seems idealistic now. I wish someone had warned me. Enough of that kind of thinking will get you killed.

"Please," I murmur, but the rest of what I want to say won't come. It's probably better this way. I glance toward the door, thinking about what's at stake if I don't make it out of here alive, wondering whether or not I can make a break for it. It's so dark out—a clear night, a moonless sky. The power is out, I gather, and it's a fair assumption. This has always been one of his favorite ways to show me what true suffering is like. That alone would make an escape difficult. I would have to set out on foot and then where would I go? Who would believe me?

"You have it too easy," he says, as though he wants to confirm my suspicions. "That's the problem nowadays. People consume everything, appreciate nothing."

He lifts me by the hair and drags me across the bedroom. I don't have to ask why. He doesn't like to argue where he sleeps, where we make love. It's one of our safe spaces, but like many things, this too is a facade. Nothing with him is safe.

"You like your comforts, but you forget nothing good comes without sacrifice."

"I haven't forgotten," I assure him, and that much is true. Sacrifice is something I know well.

He shakes his head, careful to exaggerate his movements. He wants the message he sends to sink in. "I don't know why you have to make me so angry."

I glance toward the window, thinking I see headlights, but it's wishful thinking. Then I reach up and touch the wet spot at the crown of my head. I pull my hand away, regretful I felt the need for confirmation. Instinct is enough. If only I'd realized this sooner. I didn't have to put my fingers to it to know there would be blood; the coppery scent fills the air. "It's not too bad," he huffs as he slides one hand under my armpit and hauls me up. "Come on," he presses, his fingertips digging into my skin. "Let's get you stitched up."

I follow his lead. There isn't another option. Head wounds bleed a lot, and someone's going to have to clean his mess up. If I live, that someone will be me. *This is how you stop the bleeding.* "What time is it?"

"Oh," he says, half-chuckling. "There's no need to worry about that. She's already come and gone."

I don't ask who he's referring to. I know. Everything in me sinks to the pit of my stomach. It rests there and I let it. I don't want him to see how deeply I am affected by what he's done. It's more dangerous if I let it show. But what I want to happen and what actually does, are two very different things. I know because my body tenses, as it gives over to emotion until eventually it seizes up completely. I don't mean for it to happen. It has a habit of betraying me, particularly where he is concerned. Your mind may know when something's bad for you. But the body can take a little longer. He knows where to touch me. He knows what to say. Automatic response is powerful, and like I said before, attachment is hard to break.

He shoves me hard into the wall. I guess I wasn't listening. I shouldn't have made a habit of that either. I don't feel the pain. I don't feel anything. "Ah, now look what you made me do," he huffs, running his fingers through his hair. He's staring at me as though this is the first time he's seeing me. His face is twisted. He wants me to think he's trying to work out his next move. He isn't. He's a planner, through and through.

Still, he's good at concealing what he doesn't want anyone to know. If only I'd been more like that. I wasn't. That's why I don't know if this is it, if this is the end. I only know where it began.

"We had an agreement," he reminds me. And he's right.

We did have an agreement.

That's how this all started.

READ MORE HERE: https://books2read.com/b/thesocialaffair